RELUCTANT WIFE

Although Roz's marriage to Adam Milroy wasn't unhappy, it wasn't particularly happy either—which was why Adam had suggested a temporary, informal separation. But how could Roz set about winning her husband's love when she wasn't at all sure he wanted it?

Books you will enjoy
by LINDSAY ARMSTRONG

STANDING ON THE OUTSIDE

Tallitha had been determined to forget her past when she came to Brisbane. But it seemed that working for Miles Gilmour would serve only to open the old wounds all over again, and make her vulnerable once more...

THE HEART OF THE MATTER

Clarissa had a rich and handsome husband, a beautiful daughter, and Mirrabilla, the family ranch. Yet she knew that Robert had only married her out of pity, and that he was in love with someone else. Could she manage to keep their marriage together?

THE SHADOW OF MOONLIGHT

Evan had never believed that Meredith had married his brother Leigh for any reason other than money. Now Leigh was dead and Evan had returned to the family home. But how could Meredith stand living with him?

WHEN THE NIGHT GROWS COLD

Kate's life had just about reached rock bottom when Grevil Robertson appeared on the scene and offered to save the day. But it seemed that the consequences of her acceptance were to cause Kate ever greater problems—not least Grevil himself...

RELUCTANT WIFE

BY
LINDSAY ARMSTRONG

MILLS & BOON LIMITED
ETON HOUSE   18–24 PARADISE ROAD
RICHMOND   SURREY   TW9 1SR

All the characters in this book have no existence outside the imagination of the Author, and have no relation whatsoever to anyone bearing the same name or names. They are not even distantly inspired by any individual known or unknown to the Author, and all the incidents are pure invention.

The text of this publication or any part thereof may not be reproduced or transmitted in any form or by any means, electronic or mechanical, including photocopying, recording, storage in an information retrieval system, or otherwise, without the written permission of the publisher.

This book is sold subject to the condition that it shall not, by way of trade or otherwise, be lent, resold, hired out or otherwise circulated without the prior consent of the publisher in any form of binding or cover other than that in which it is published and without a similar condition including this condition being imposed on the subsequent purchaser.

First published in Great Britain 1987 by Mills & Boon Limited

© Lindsay Armstrong 1987

*Australian copyright 1987
Philippine copyright 1987
This edition 1987*

ISBN 0 263 75777 3

*Set in Times 10 on 11¾ pt.
07-0787-48460*

*Computer typeset by SB Datagraphics,
Colchester, Essex*

*Printed and bound in Great Britain by
Collins, Glasgow*

CHAPTER ONE

ROZ MILROY tensed as her bedroom door opened, but it was Milly Barker who stuck her curly head around it to say, 'Adam's on his way, Roz. His office just rang. Can I get you anything in the meantime? Jeanette says you're ready.'

'No, thanks, Milly, I'll come down . . .' Roz hesitated briefly. 'On second thoughts, I might have a drink up here. If you wouldn't mind,' she added.

'Yours to command,' Milly said cheerfully, revealing all of her small person in the doorway. She was middle-aged, wore her brown curls cropped short and an enormous pair of spectacles through which she appeared to view the world myopically, but in the two years of their association, Roz had come to realise that very little escaped Milly Barker. She also ran the Milroy household superbly. 'What would you like? I must say that colour looks gorgeous on you, and Jeanette has excelled herself with your hair—oh, damn! There's the phone again. A sherry?'

'I think I'd like a gin and tonic,' said Roz a shade tentatively, almost as if she expected to encounter opposition to this request, but Milly merely waved a hand and dashed out.

A few minutes later the gin and tonic arrived via Jeanette, who said earnestly, 'That was Mr Milroy's office on the phone again. Something came up just as he was leaving, would you believe!' She looked at Roz indignantly. 'But he'll still be here in good time, his secretary said. Here's your drink.'

'Thank you, Jeanette.' Roz accepted the glass with a smile. 'I suppose the place is humming downstairs?'

'You're not wrong,' Jeanette replied, her plain, round young face creasing ruefully. 'I don't know where to put myself. You were right to stay up here, were you ever! Milly is convinced the extra help she got in all have ten thumbs and two left feet. What we need is for Mr Milroy to come home. He always calms things down.'

Roz regarded Jeanette wryly and wondered why it didn't irritate her more, the fact that Jeanette thought the sun shone out of Adam Milroy and never attempted to hide it. But then from the time Jeanette had been employed as a permanent live-in offsider to Milly and also to look after Roz's wardrobe, they'd formed a bond of friendship, possibly because they'd been much of an age and both shy and raw. But anyway, how could you get irritated with such honesty and devotion?

'Perhaps *I* ought to be able to calm things down,' she suggested.

'Oh no!' Jeanette looked quite shocked. 'You don't have to worry your head about the *preparations*. It's your birthday tonight and it's Milly's job and she's really very good at it. Why, she could handle double the amount of people and not turn a hair—often does—but family nights, we-ell, you know how particular Mr Milroy's mother is, and his sister, Mrs Whatney. It's as if we're on trial,' Jeanette added, rolling her eyes.

Roz grimaced, but Jeanette had only paused for breath.

'Whereas *your* job normally when we entertain is to be the hostess, and that's no easy job, I'm sure. I know I couldn't do it, but it's very important to Mr Milroy to have you at his side especially serene and poised and beautiful. You're like the jewel of his house,' Jeanette said fervently.

Roz had to smile. 'It's very kind of you to say so, Jeanette. In fact I don't know what I'd do without you,' she added obscurely.

But Jeanette assured her she would do quite fine, then took herself off downstairs to help Milly.

Roz took her drink over to the window and pondered the fact that if Milly and Jeanette felt as if they were on trial on family nights, it was nothing to how she felt.

The sun was setting, but the grounds around the house were already lit up and it was an impressive sight—the floodlit swimming pool and tennis court and the long sweep of lawn that led down to the stables. The house itself was two-storeyed and had a graceful veranda running right round. Above the sloping veranda roof all the bedrooms in the upper storey had long casement windows, which afforded different views of the eighty-acre property known as Little Werrington.

'Why little?' Roz had asked Adam once.

'It's named after the family property out west which we lost after a succession of droughts, slumps in beef prices—possibly too many cooks spoiling the broth,' he'd said a shade drily. 'But it was eighty thousand acres.'

'Is that where you grew up?'

'Yes. And most of the rest of us.'

'Do you miss it?'

'No. It was ... another era of my life, I guess.'

Just as I am, she'd thought.

And she found herself remembering that thought on the night of her birthday—her twenty-first birthday—as she stared over the darkening acres of Little Werrington, set so conveniently in the rolling landscape of Pimpama, half-way between Brisbane and the Gold Coast, so that it was only half an hour's drive to get to Brisbane where Adam had his headquarters, or half an hour in the other direction to get to the surf and the sand and the increasingly elegant shopping and exotic nightlife of Surfers' Paradise. Yet you could be forgiven for thinking you were living in the heart of the country at Pimpama.

'The best of both worlds,' she murmured out loud, and turned away from the window to stare at herself in the mirror in the fading daylight.

The dress she wore was a soft, glowing ruby red with a full long skirt, a fitted bodice and a small ruffled frill skimming the tops of her breasts and circling her shoulders. With it she wore a diamond and gold bracelet on her right wrist, a present that morning from Adam, as were the diamond earrings she wore—as was everything she possessed.

Her high, slender-heeled shoes matched the dress exactly, and so did her engagement ring, an oval ruby surrounded by diamonds.

She thought absently as she gazed at her reflection that Milly was right, it wasn't so much the dress but the colour against her skin, the ruby red against her fairness, that made the impact. And for that Jeanette had to take the credit. She had sorted through endless swatches of material and picked it personally. She had also chosen the style, saying, 'Mr Milroy doesn't like you in anything too fussy or slinky.'

She was right, Roz mused. Mr Milroy likes rich simplicity, and what Mr Milroy says goes, particularly for the *second* Mrs Milroy. I wonder ...

But she sighed suddenly and sipped her drink, knowing it was futile to speculate on that subject. And instead, as she thought of turning on the lamps in her beautiful bedroom but didn't, she found herself wishing she'd been spared Jeanette's words earlier on what her role in life was, but not because they weren't true. It was her role to be pampered and carefully instructed in all the finer things so that she could be a fine hostess, always to be beautifully groomed, always to be watched and guarded against getting overwrought. Her role to be brought out and admired, rather like a jewel in her husband's house, but ...

A sound behind her made her jump and spill some of her drink, and she swung round and peered through the gloom. 'Adam?'

'Yes. Why are you in the dark?'

'No—no reason,' she said with a catch in her voice. She heard a click and the central light sprang on, causing her to blink in the radiance.

'Well,' said Adam Milroy, leaning his wide shoulders against the doorframe, 'you look stunning, Roz.'

'So everyone keeps telling me, but thank you,' she said jerkily, and their gazes clashed briefly across the wide expanse of mushroom carpet before she lowered a veil of carefully darkened lashes over her smoky blue gaze.

He straightened. 'What's wrong?'

Roz drew a quivering breath and turned away. 'Nothing,' she said flatly, and sipped her drink, glancing down anxiously at her dress to see if she'd spilt any of it on it. Then, although she had heard nothing, she shivered inwardly and knew he'd crossed the carpet silently with that lazy, easy grace and was standing behind her like the Prince of Darkness she had once romantically, as a teenager, thought of him—for that matter still sometimes did, despite being twenty-one and despite knowing him in the biblical sense.

She turned round suddenly, and he was there as she'd

guessed, tall and dark, her senior by some sixteen years and several lifetimes of experience. A man who was a formidable opponent but with a lightning sense of humour and a brilliant, crooked smile that sometimes took her breath away, sometimes made her feel dull and slow. But then experience had taught *her* some things, hadn't it? That to fight him was hopeless, for one thing ...

'I'm all right,' she said, and was surprised at the steadiness of her voice. 'Really. Well, just nerves, perhaps.'

He said nothing for a moment, then, 'I thought you'd got over that. Especially with the family.'

Roz shrugged.

'What's that?' he asked, looking at her drink.

'Gin and tonic.'

Adam raised his dark eyebrows quizzically. 'Dutch courage?'

'There's nothing wrong with it, is there?'

He looked at her consideringly. 'Not so long ago you were hard to persuade to even have a pre-dinner sherry.'

This was true, and she still usually only drank wine with meals and generally only a glass at that. But she said with a tight little smile, 'I'm not going to get *drunk*. I just—perhaps I just felt like breaking out. After all, I'm eligible for the key of the door now, aren't I? So if I feel like choosing my own drink,' her voice rose, ' ... what are you doing?'

'Getting rid of it,' he said calmly, and took the glass from her. 'I'd be surprised if you even like it.' He put the glass down and turned back to her to say softly, 'If you really wanted to exercise your—key of the door powers, I can think of a much better way.' His dark gaze flickered over her from head to toe, from her upswept hairdo that gleamed so fair beneath the light, her oval face, deep blue eyes and straight little nose, at the ivory-tinted skin of her arms and shoulders, the slenderness of her waist beneath the ruby material—and back to her face again.

'Wh-what do you mean?' she asked unevenly. 'You don't surely . . .?' She tailed off, her eyes widening.

'Why not?' Adam said lazily but with a glint in his dark eyes. 'It would be a very adult thing to do. Particularly,' he went on barely audibly, 'if you could persuade yourself to admit that contrary to all expectations, for some strange reason I've yet to fathom, you like me making love to you as opposed to simply enduring it. Or did you think I was unaware of it, my lovely Rozalinda? Unaware that it's getting harder and harder for you to lie in my arms as passively as you used to, before the . . . possibilities of it were known to you?'

Her lips parted and her cheeks grew hot with a lovely delicate flush of colour, but her eyes darkened with something like anger.

But Adam only looked amused and lifted a hand idly to trace the outline of her mouth with one finger. 'It's hard to have to admit you can be wrong about things, whatever the reason, I know,' he said with gentle mockery. 'But I've generally found it's the best policy. Also,' he added meditatively, and his hand moved down to slide the ruby ruffle resting on the point of her shoulder a fraction lower, 'wouldn't it be terribly daring and grown-up to snap your fingers at everyone due to descend on us shortly, to keep them waiting for a little while and come to bed with me now?'

'*No!* No,' Roz said raggedly, and jerked away from him. 'Anyway, you're only teasing me!' she said hotly as he laughed softly.

His eyebrows lifted. 'Try me,' he invited.

'I . . . it would take me ages to get ready again . . .' She broke off in confusion and feeling foolish.

'If that's what's worrying you,' he said wryly, making her feel even more foolish, 'I'm sure Jeanette could do an express job on you and . . .'

'It took her an hour just to do my hair,' Roz interrupted with strained but deliberately gathered composure. Her very own weapon against Adam and one that she was gradually perfecting—she had thought until tonight had let her down, and for some reason Adam himself had apparently decided to test it, whereas he normally only acknowledged it with an ironic look but mostly ignored it. But the trick is to keep at it, she thought drily. 'I'd hate to disappoint her, not to mention possibly shocking her rigid,' she said.

'Oh, do you think you would?' he countered, and he was suddenly no longer laughing or even looking amused. 'I suspect you shock more easily than Jeanette, Roz. In fact I think she'd be delighted. I'm sure she's a romantic at heart.'

'Which I am not?' Roz asked coolly.

'No,' he said thoughtfully. 'And in some danger of becoming a virtuous bore . . .'

It happened before she could stop herself—a shockingly sharp little explosion of sound as she reached up and hit him. 'I h-hate you!' she stammered through clenched teeth, her face scarlet now and her eyes burning, but she also backed away a step a bare moment later.

If she expected some physical retaliation it was not what she got, however. Adam's mouth tightened and he lifted a hand to explore the red mark on his cheek. Then he reached across and grasped her wrist and her heart started to pound, but all he said very evenly was, 'I wouldn't do that again, Roz.'

'Then don't provoke me!' she retorted angrily, but in her heart she was still half afraid of what he might do but determined not to let him know it. And she tilted her chin defiantly at him.

He surprised her. He said, 'That's better, actually,' with a wry little smile twisting his lips.

She stared at him. 'What do you mean?'

Adam shrugged and grinned. 'Provided you keep your fists to yourself,' he curled her hand into a fist and covered it with his own, 'provided you do that,' he looked into her stormy blue eyes, 'I prefer to see you in a rage than cold and polite and haughty. But there's just one thing you shouldn't forget. We made a bargain for various reasons, my dear Roz. One which I've stuck to. Perhaps you ought to remember that.'

'I've stuck to it too! I . . .'

'Have you?' he said drily.

'Yes!'

'Or would it be more accurate to say—stuck to it but hated it?' he queried, his eyes now glinting with impatience.

'No,' she whispered, her lips trembling. 'I mean . . .'

'Then spare me your pride and your holier-than-thou looks, Roz,' he put in sardonically. 'Or I might be tempted to take you down a peg or two—oh, in the nicest possible way,' he added softly and with a look that brought the blood to her cheeks again.

'If you mean what I think you mean,' Roz said stiffly, 'there's nothing you can do to me that hasn't . . .' She broke off and bit her lip.

He smiled faintly. 'You don't really believe that, do you?'

They stared at each other.

'Well then,' he said drily, 'it's definitely time I showed you otherwise, my love.'

'I'm not your . . .' But he cut her off with an irritable gesture.

'Let's not go into *that* now, Roz.'

'You brought the subject up,' she said defensively.

'Yes,' he agreed, 'because you're as tense as a piano wire and looking as if your heart is full of tears again, for nothing. Believe me, Roz, the alternative to this would have been something you really wouldn't have liked. I thought you understood and accepted that. But now it seems as if I've become some sort of an ogre.'

Roz stared up into his dark eyes, then her gaze fell away guiltily. 'I'm sorry,' she said huskily, 'if I seem ungrateful after all you've done for me. I don't mean to be—I'm not.' Her shoulders slumped. 'And I'm sorry if I've been a fool and I'll try to make amends . . .' She blushed suddenly and for the first time considered that she might sound virtuous and boring and holier-than-thou.

He said, 'If you could just relax it might help. It can't all be hard labour, surely?'

'No . . .'

'Then forget this conversation and concentrate for once on enjoying yourself tonight. It is your party, and even if my family are all mad, I'm sure they'd like to see you happy. Which reminds me, I'd better get ready. Finish that,' he added over his shoulder, gesturing towards her drink as he walked across to the interleading door to his bedroom. 'You're right, at twenty-one you are entitled to break out.'

Roz watched him go, her eyes wide and wary and confused.

They hadn't originally had separate bedrooms, but it

had seemed to be a good idea because Adam often worked late and she had trouble sleeping, so he didn't have to disturb her if she was asleep. But now, suddenly, they seemed to represent more to her than that. Now they represented the deep rift in their marriage which had been exposed to the light tonight.

She sighed and turned away and her eyes fell on the glass of gin and tonic, and she sighed again because she hadn't liked it, and the last thing she wanted to do was finish it.

Curiously, she did enjoy herself without quite knowing how or why, but she suspected that her state of mind had become too much to bear, so she'd switched off, in a manner of speaking. Then also, she was surprised and touched by the gifts she received and the warmth of the congratulations and the fact that everyone seemed to be really happy and determined to make it a happy, memorable night for her. She'd always thought she was a bit of a disappointment and knew she was something of an enigma to the Milroy clan.

But although Flavia, Adam's mother, subjected her to the usual fleeting scrutiny directed squarely at her waistline, the gaiety was obviously infectious, and anyway, Roz knew that Flavia was as proud as punch of all her grandchildren so far and could be expected to be eager to add her eldest son's children to the growing score.

Flavia Milroy was Italian, had borne Adam when she was nineteen and subsequently five more little Milroys at irregular intervals—to the embarrassment of Adam's father's side of the family, all two-and-a-half-children-at-the-most families themselves, and aggressively Anglo-Saxon, as was often the case with colonial offshoots of the real thing.

'Never,' Adam had said to her once, 'allow my family to get to you. They're all mad, on both sides, and I disregard them.'

He might disregard their opinions, Roz had decided, but he certainly provided for them very well, which probably accounted for their eagerness to meet under his auspices despite their sometimes acute differences. And she often wished she'd known Adam's father, Charles Milroy, not only as a clue to his eldest son but as a guide to this melting pot of a family which he had instigated by marrying Adam's mother.

In fact the sheer weight of numbers had made Roz, an only child herself and an orphan, dizzy at first, until Adam's cousin Margaret had taken pity on her and drawn her a family tree. Margaret was widowed with two children, Amy and Richard, eighteen and twenty.

But Margaret had gone further, in her forthright manner, and said, 'Now, there's one tour de force in this family, and that's Adam, as you might have gathered. Anyone who can make himself a million from nothing before he's thirty has to be someone to be reckoned with, but then even when we were all kids Adam was a force to be reckoned with. But there are several minor forces too, and it might help you to know about them. Aunt Flavia is one. She runs an unparalleled spy network and knows *everything* that goes on. Don't ask me how, but she does.'

'Even in your side of the family?' asked Roz.

'Even there,' Margaret said ruefully. 'You see, when Charles married her, he and his two sisters, of which one was my mother and the other Aunt Elspeth, had inherited Werrington jointly. They all lived there and worked it together—that's what Charles brought Flavia home to after a whirlwind romance in Rome, and that's how we all grew up together and became so engrossed in each other.'

'That must have been rather hard for her.'

'It had to be. She could barely speak English when she got tossed in with the Milroys, she had no relations of her own to fall back on, she must have been homesick, not to mention . . . other obstacles,' Margaret smiled.

'Oh?'

'Mmm . . . my mother got on well with her and personally I've always admired and liked her, but Aunt Elspeth—well, let's just say they took an instant dislike to each other and used to have some jolly old dust-ups. But to get back—the second minor force is Lucia, Adam's sister and the eldest daughter.'

'I . . .' Roz stopped.

'Find her hard to like?' enquired Margaret. 'Don't worry, we all do. Although I must say—or perhaps I shouldn't—but as a girl she wasn't quite so . . .' she gestured. 'But anyway,' she went on after a moment, 'she gets around now as if she was the supreme arbiter of all the taste and elegance in the family, not to mention its first lady—by the way, that's your role now, and don't let her tell you any different. But she really likes to think she has great power of influence over us and she's not always terribly ethical about it, I'm afraid. And the third force,' she said slowly, 'is about to be born. Well, she's already born, but I don't think anyone has realised her potential yet. I'm talking about Nicky.'

Nicola, universally known as Nicky, was Adam's youngest sister and the baby of the family at nineteen. 'But she's a honey,' Roz said bewilderedly.

'I'm not disputing that. I've just got the uncomfortable feeling that Nicky will move heaven and earth one day to get what she wants whether it's what she should have or not, and that even Adam will find her hard to control.'

'I think Adam's really fond of her. He sort of stands in as her father.'

'That might be the problem—how fond he is of her,' Margaret said cryptically, but then she had shrugged and gone on briskly, 'I hope you don't mind me filling you in like this but you looked totally confused at the last family get-together, and not only about who was who but all the cross-currents as well.'

'I was,' said Roz ruefully, then a thought struck her. 'Isn't it odd that all the minor forces, as you call them, are female?'

Margaret had smiled with genuine humour. 'There's at least one more, and she's on our side of the family. Wait until you see Aunt Elspeth in action! But I can tell you one other thing, when you produce a son and heir for Adam, they'll not be able to hold a candle to you, Roz...'

The irony of that last remark was to stay with Roz over the ensuing months, and not only because she had no desire to be first lady of the family. And when Margaret had made her disclosures, Roz had been tempted to ask her about Adam's first wife, but found herself unable to broach a subject that seemed to be totally taboo. She'd also treated Margaret's confidences with some wariness and tried to stop herself from making judgements based on them. But it was obvious that Adam liked and respected his cousin Margaret, and he certainly did everything he could for the fatherless Amy and Richard, even to employing Richard. But she'd gradually grown to see the truth of Margaret's assessments of the family, except for one. For the life of her she couldn't imagine where Nicky fitted in as a minor force.

Like Adam and Angelo—Angelo was the fifth of Flavia's children and Nicky's immediate elder, a dashing young blade of twenty-three—Nicky had inherited her mother's dark good looks, although some of the Milroys were fair and Lucia was a striking Titian-haired goddess with a magnificent figure, although the proud mother of three. But Nicky had a bright, sunny personality, and although there had been some recent drama associated with her it had been more Flavia's drama. Nicky had wanted to go flatting with two university friends, which seemed quite a normal aspiration for a nineteen-year-old—as Adam had pointed out to his mother. Also that Nicky would still be in the same city, not on the other side of the moon.

But Flavia had found the decision hard to make, and Roz had pointed out to Adam that it couldn't be easy losing the last of your children from home. He had replied with a slight smile that his mother was a very resilient person, she must be to have been torn from her own family so young, survived the Milroys, coped with being widowed fairly young and rendered nearly destitute for a time. And that she would make the necessary adjustments, he had no doubt.

On the night of her twenty-first birthday, after dinner had been successfully concluded to Milly's patent relief and Roz was sitting with Flavia and Lucia as the band struck up, she glanced at her mother-in-law, and couldn't help admiring her because she had made the necessary adjustments as Adam had predicted, just as she'd coped rather marvellously with being ousted from Little Werrington two years ago by a complete stranger, something Roz had always felt guilty about—but then Flavia had taken that step herself.

Then, as more dancers drifted on to the floor, Nicky looking bewitching in pink taffeta and talking nineteen to the dozen to Richard as they danced, and Angelo with a gorgeous young blonde in his arms, Flavia said out of the blue, 'I so hope those two babies don't get any ideas about anything. It would not be suitable.'

'Angelo's not a baby, Mamma,' Lucia said languidly. 'Ideas about what?'

'Nothing. Nothing,' Flavia said hastily, and turned to Roz with a smile. 'Now see what you have started, Rozalinda!'

'I have?'

'Why, yes! A vogue in twenty-first birthday parties. Let's see, there is Richard to come and pretty soon, then Amy, then Nicky, not to mention my dear sister-in-law's eldest grandchild Julian—I'm quite sure Elspeth would have her nose severely broken if Adam did not . . .'

'Not broken, Mamma,' Lucia interrupted. 'How many times do I have to tell you? Out of joint is the correct term, and anyway . . .'

'Lucia,' Flavia, who was petite and plump now but must have been a raving beauty as a girl, Roz had decided, because even now she had perfect skin, flashing eyes, long dark hair and exquisite hands as well as exquisite taste in clothes, drew herself up in her chair and continued, 'ever since I have spoken this peculiar language I have *referred* to broken noses and everyone has known exactly what I have meant, so I will not change this late in life. Please bear with me and refrain from correcting me in public or in private or anywhere else!'

Lucia raised her eyes heavenwards, and Roz turned away to hide her smile, for it had occurred to her before that although Flavia and Lucia spent a lot of time in each other's company, even Lucia's mamma found her rather a cross to bear.

But Lucia remained unperturbed. 'And anyway——' she went on—but Adam appeared before them and took his mother away for a dance, to her delight.

And hard on his heels came Angelo to Roz's rescue, having discarded his gorgeous blonde for the time being.

'Thought I just had to rescue you from Lucia and Mamma,' he said with a grin. 'But in reality I've been dying to dance with you, Roz. You always look beautiful, but tonight it's gone beyond words, and I'm so sorry Adam met you first. I suppose you know I'm hiding a broken heart beneath this false air of gaiety?' He twirled her round to the music and her skirt belled out and she found herself laughing up at him.

'So I'd noticed!' she teased him.

'Because I dance with others . . .'

'She's lovely!'

'Only for consolation . . .' Angelo broke off and stared at her. Then he said eagerly, 'Do you really think so, Roz?'

'Yes, I do. And I spoke to her earlier and thought she was nice as well as lovely.'

'If only I could get the rest of the family to agree with you! But I know them well enough to know they don't.'

'Well——' Roz hesitated, 'I'm sure they wouldn't disagree that she's good-looking and nice, but you must admit you fall in love about every two months on average.'

Angelo looked mortally offended, then burst out laughing and they laughed together companionably. 'I suppose that's true, but I've got a feeling about this one. Only I'm quite sure they'll think up another excuse—that I'm too young to be thinking of marriage or . . . God knows what!'

'Probably,' Roz agreed ruefully.

'Oh well,' said Angelo philosophically, 'let's not spoil

your birthday with my problems, darling Roz, in fact I tell you what.'

'What?'

'Now that we've got dinner out of the way, I thought I might liven the proceedings up a bit. I couldn't *bear* it,' he said intensely, 'to degenerate into one of Lucia's polite, bloody boring soirées.'

'Well . . .' Roz looked around for Adam.

'But I promise I won't go overboard! Hey! It is your *twenty*-first birthday, not your forty-first!'

Roz giggled. 'All right. What did you have in mind—no, better not tell me,' she said wryly. 'Then I can claim some innocence!'

Over an hour later, when she had stopped dancing but only to get her breath back, she felt a hand on her shoulder and turned to see Adam behind her, and she immediately looked guilty because it was the first time she'd even thought of him in that time.

'Well,' he said, 'you're enjoying yourself after all. I'm glad.'

'Yes, I am. I . . . it's got quite lively, hasn't it?' she said breathlessly.

'Yes. I wonder who we have to thank for that—I suspect Angelo. I saw him in close conversation with the band some time ago.'

'My lips are sealed,' said Roz with a little laugh.

'I see,' Adam said gravely. 'Did you also tell him to dim the lights?'

'They were all his own . . .' She broke off ruefully because he was laughing down at her. 'Then you don't mind?' she asked after a moment.

'Why should I? Everyone's enjoying themselves. Even the Whatneys,' he said with an ironic little bow as Lucia and her fair, handsome barrister husband danced past. 'What's more,' he added, staring through the throng with his lips twitching, 'Aunt Elspeth is up and dancing.'

'No! Who with?'

'Richard. He's leading her around very deferentially and she's loving every minute of it, although she's trying to do a waltz. By the way, may I have this dance with you, Mrs Milroy?'

'Of course,' she smiled, and moved into his arms obediently. But the band chose that moment to take pity on the older members of the clan and slid into a slow, dreamy number.

Adam pulled her closer and she stumbled, which was unusual for her—she was a good dancer and in her last year at school, she and her boyfriend had won a prize at the end of the course offered by the school. She was also used to dancing with Adam, which made it more unusual, and although he didn't comment on it, it was a mocking little look he directed down at her as she regained her rhythm.

She flushed, because she knew why it had happened to her and knew he knew why—it was the feel of his body against hers, strong and hard. She closed her eyes and broke into a sweat, thanking God for the dimmed lights, because the contact had not only made her stumble but remember with extraordinary clarity the last time he had made love to her. It had been a few nights ago, a rather windy night, and the curtains had billowed in so that the room had been dark and alternately flooded with moonlight as she had lain on the bed with Adam beside her propped up on one elbow and idly touching her breasts, plucking her nipples, stroking, cupping, while she fought a battle she fought often these days and lost frequently. Lost this time with a gasping little breath as she had arched her pale, slender body towards him in a moment of moonlight.

She swallowed but danced steadily as she remembered what had followed, and beneath the ruby red of her gown and the lacy cups of her strapless bra, her nipples tingled just as if his hands were on them, and stood up.

She never knew what gave her the composure to keep dancing, to tear her mind away from that vision of herself lying in Adam's arms afterwards exhausted and with her body dewed with sweat but quivering with pleasure. Or what gave her the composure, when Adam asked her suddenly what she was thinking, to shrug and say—nothing.

Then, to her consternation, a spotlight came on and found her and Adam unerringly, and the band slid into a drum roll, then a stirring rendition of Happy Birthday. And Roz thought she'd never felt more naked in life.

'Oh!' she breathed, but Adam bent his dark head and kissed her and said as his lips left hers, 'And many, many more, Roz.'

'Oh, thank you,' she managed to whisper, consumed by guilt. 'I didn't expect . . . I mean . . .'

'Angelo and I did some conniving of our own,' he murmured.

'Angelo is . . . you're both very . . .' But she was engulfed then and kissed and embraced by everyone, including all the children, who had been having a party of their own under Jeanette's supervision, and finally Jeanette and Milly.

'I don't know what to say!' she said at last. 'Thank you all so much. I . . .'

But there was no need for her to say anything, because the band broke into 'For She's a Jolly Good Fellow', and everyone sang as if they really meant it and toasted her with champagne, and the thought struck her that they must like her. They really must, to be looking so fond and sounding so sincere. She glanced at Adam, still at her side, but he had turned to talk to his mother, who was absolutely bubbling with good spirits, and the feeling of guilt was there again alongside the warmth and happiness.

Jeanette came upstairs with Roz when the party was over.

'You don't need to. I can put myself to bed,' Roz protested, but Jeanette merely looked wise and said it was part of her job.

'Your mother trained you well,' murmured Roz. Jeanette's mother had held a similar position with one of Flavia's friends, and it was Flavia who had suggested to Adam that Roz might need some assistance and recommended Jeanette. But in her heart of hearts, although she was so fond of Jeanette, Roz thought it was a waste of her talents, and she fully intended to steer her towards a dress designing course as soon as her mother felt she was old enough to be unleashed on the wide world.

But Jeanette herself took her responsibilities very seriously, as she demonstrated yet again by insisting, once Roz was changed into a long, filmy white nightgown, on unpinning her hair and brushing it out.

'It's so beautiful,' she said as she slid the brush through the silky fair mass that came well below Roz's shoulders, 'it would be a shame not to look after it properly. There! Doesn't that feel better?'

Roz regarded her gravely in the mirror, then said with her eyes twinkling, 'Yes, Mum.'

'Well . . .'

Roz relented. 'No, it does. Thank you. I think I told you earlier that I don't know what I'd do without you.'

'Oh, bosh!' Jeanette protested forcefully, but she was laughing herself. Then she looked around to see if she'd forgotten to put anything away, but the mushroom and dusky pink bedroom was perfectly tidy with the coverlet and sheet pulled down neatly on the big bed. 'There,' she said. 'Will you be able to sleep? Should I get you something? Mr Milroy's here, but . . .'

'No, I'll be fine, Jeanette. Goodnight.'

But once she was alone, Roz hesitated before getting into bed and wondered whether Adam had come up yet. Their interleading door was closed.

Then she shrugged and switched off all the lamps. She sat on the bed with one leg drawn up and her chin resting on it, pondering on a strange night and her equally strange mixture of feelings. But her overriding thought, she discovered, was how Adam would be next. Sardonic and mocking as he had been in their first encounter of the evening? But then he'd been apparently happy to see her happy later. And how would she be? What would she feel?

She bit her lip, and the door between her bedroom and Adam's opened.

CHAPTER TWO

Roz turned her head so that her cheek was resting on her knee and watched as her husband came slowly across to the bed. He had taken off his jacket and tie and his shirt was open at the throat, the sleeves unbuttoned and pushed up a little, and his dark hair lay across his forehead as if he had just raked a hand through it.

A swathe of light streamed in from his room and their eyes met. 'Not tired?' he asked after a moment.

'Yes,' she whispered.

'But you can't sleep?'

She moved. 'I haven't tried. Have you come to ... to ...?' She broke off awkwardly.

He waited, but she could only colour foolishly. Then he said, 'Would you like me to, Roz?' His dark gaze was sombre and very direct.

She raised her head and looked away, but something seemed to clear in her mind and she said with an effort, 'I'd like to thank you for everything. And also,' her voice sank, 'try to make up for being ... idiotic. So yes, I would like you to.'

Adam was silent for so long she felt her nerves tightening almost unbearably.

But it got worse as he said drily, 'Well, that's a new twist. How do you think you'll feel about *that* in the morning?'

Her eyes widened. 'What do you mean?'

A smile that didn't reach his eyes twisted his lips. 'I

mean, do you think it will ease the way you normally feel? Will you be able to . . . say, see it in another light? As if you were paying your dues, so it was *different*?'

She stared at him and dimly began to realise she had made an awful mistake.

'Roz?'

She licked her lips and a pulse started to beat erratically at the base of her throat.

Adam made an impatient sound as she tried to speak, but twisted her hands together instead.

'Do you think I don't know how you feel in the mornings?' he queried harshly. 'You hate yourself and you hate me, although God knows why. But you see,' he smiled grimly, 'I know you better than you know yourself, I sometimes think, and being *grateful* isn't going to make it any more acceptable to you for long, Roz. Nor me. I'd far rather you were honest with me. In fact, that's the only thing I'm prepared to accept from you now, Roz. So goodnight, my dear, but of course if you can't sleep don't hesitate to call and I'll get you something.'

She stumbled off the bed. 'You're right—I do. I hate you!' she stammered, but clenched her fists because she knew without a doubt that he wouldn't be nearly so gentle with her this time if she hit him. And she was shocked that she should want to again, and so soon. What's happening to me? she wondered despairingly.

Then she realised that he was waiting for her to go on and watching her carefully but quite dispassionately. And that the light from his bedroom was striking through her nightgown so that it looked about as substantial as moonlight and so that her high, pointed breasts, tiny waist, hips and slender legs were outlined clearly.

She turned away abruptly and defensively, and

instantly felt incredibly foolish. Because it wasn't as if he didn't know every square inch of her body, hadn't handled it with those long, strong *expert* hands, and much, much more.

Roz closed her eyes and felt a flood of heat suffuse her from head to toe at the way he could make her feel just by touching her, just by looking at her, if one were to be honest. And how she could fall asleep in his arms afterwards as if she never suffered from recurring nightmares and sometimes did anything to keep herself awake so that her insomnia had become a vicious circle *but* . . .

'All right,' she swung back to face him, 'so what if everything you say is true? I can't help it and I can't change it. Don't think I haven't tried—I have. The thing is, if you really must know, I feel like a . . . like a *kept* woman, and I thought it might be appreciated if I earned my keep for a change . . . Adam!' She took a step backwards in sudden fright, but he made no move, although his mouth had set pale and taut and a nerve flickered suddenly in his jaw.

But then he drawled, 'My, my, you have grown up, Roz! Two years ago I doubt if you'd have known what that meant.'

'I wasn't *that* naïve,' she said, flushing. 'But I'm sorry, I shouldn't have said that. It was ridiculous and melodramatic.'

'But honest.'

'You said that's what you wanted,' she whispered.

'Go on.'

She lifted her shoulders in a helpless little gesture. 'We both know why you married me. Because I was in so much trouble . . .'

'Yes, you were, Roz,' he interrupted, but his voice had changed and he looked suddenly more weary than anything else.

'You don't have to keep reminding me ...'

'Do I do that? I can't remember referring to it constantly. It's *you* who keeps remembering my iniquities. How I married you to get my hands on a horse, how I tore you away from the love of your life ...'

'Adam' she broke in anguishedly, 'I never believed that about Nimmitabel or Michael. But it *was* a marriage of ... of ...'

'Convenience?' he supplied sardonically.

'*Yes*. I had all those problems. You said that after your first marriage you'd grown cynical about love, etcetera, but you wanted a family ...'

'I also told you I wanted you, Roz,' he said quietly.

'It's not the same thing,' she whispered. 'You thought you could mould me into the perfect wife, didn't you? But what I've really become is the perfect hostess. And to make it all worse, it seems as if I'm not going to be able to provide you with a family either. I ... I don't know why,' she said jerkily, 'but I really regret that. Perhaps it would have solved a lot of our problems, but anyway, I think you'd have made a good father. But it's not too late for *you*. You have only to let me go.'

'Go?' He looked at her and laughed. 'Go where? Perhaps I should have mentioned this before, but Michael Howard is married now.'

Her mouth dropped open. 'How do you know that?'

He regarded her stunned blue eyes and shrugged. 'It's not important, and he's two years older now. What is important is that that avenue is no longer open to you, in case you've been dreaming romantically of it, my dear Roz.'

She gasped. 'I . . .'

'Hate me? So you keep telling me,' Adam said leisurely. 'But I'm afraid it's something we're going to have to live with.'

'D-do you know what I think?' she stammered in her anger. 'I think you might have grown cynical and distrustful of women, but you still can't bear to think of even one of them being unaffected by you . . .'

'Unaffected?' he drawled with a lift of his eyebrows.

'You *know* what I mean. You're determined to make me fall in love with you—that's the problem!'

But if she thought she could shock him or even anger him, she was mistaken. Because he stared down at her for a moment, then his lips twisted into a cool smile and a genuine spark of amusement lit his eyes as he said, 'Possibly. I never could resist a challenge. Well, now we've sorted all that out, should we go to bed? Together or separately—you choose, Roz.'

Then he laughed at her expression, dropped a brief kiss on her forehead, murmured, 'So be it,' and walked through to his bedroom, closing the door behind him.

It was a long time before Roz fell asleep, and then only to wake up sweating but shivering and only by the greatest effort of will forced herself to calm down.

And as the dawn broke she was thinking of Michael Howard and wondering who he had married with a haunting sense of sadness, but not, as Adam imagined, because she had been indulging in romantic daydreams about a reunion with Mike. That was impossible anyway, she knew, but she had more than once wished she could have explained things to him.

She twisted restlessly and knew she would start to feel suffocated if she stayed in bed one moment longer.

The air was clear and dewy and fresh as she arrived at the stables, and not a soul had stirred when she had let herself out of the house and stolen across the lawn. But the stables were a hive of activity, and the first person she bumped into was Adam's trainer.

'Well, I thought you'd be sleeping in this morning, Roz,' he said with a grin. 'Good party?'

'Great, thanks, Les. Have you worked Nimmitabel yet?'

'She's just about to go out. Want to ride her?'

'If you wouldn't mind.'

'Now why would I mind? You're one of the best track riders I've seen. Just wish you were on the permanent staff. Anyway, she's yours.' Then he turned businesslike. 'Three furlongs, three-quarter pace this morning, Roz, and give her a good warm up—but watch her, she's fresh.'

'Thanks, Les,' Roz said warmly. 'Will I work with another horse?'

'No, take her out on her own. I want to watch her action. Hey, Jake,' he called, and the stable jockey just about to mount an excited-looking brown filly, turned and touched his cap. 'Mrs Milroy'll take her,' said Les.

'Morning, ma'am,' said Jake. 'She's a bit of a handful this morning.'

'Good,' said Roz, 'that's just what I need.' And she sprang lightly up into the saddle, adjusted her cap while Jake held the filly and Les altered the irons. Then she was off.

Twenty minutes later she was back in the stable yard with her cheeks glowing and her eyes bright, and even Les, who didn't display much emotion about a horse unless it was really called for, was shaking his head—a sign of enthusiasm. 'Goes like a bird, Roz. I reckon she'll be everything your grandfather expected of her and more. She does it so easily. Long time since I've seen a galloper like her.'

Roz slid off Nimmitabel to a little round of applause from everyone watching. 'Thanks!' she called breathlessly. 'Can I wash her down and put her away? When do you think she'll be ready for her first start, by the way?'

'A month or so,' said Les. 'Barring accidents and shin soreness, etcetera, but you don't have to . . .'

'I want to,' Roz said firmly.

'But Adam . . .'

'What Adam doesn't know can't hurt him. Come on, Bel, it's just you and me this morning, as it used to be,' Roz said softly to the horse, and led her away.

But as she worked on the horse, walking her to cool her off, hosing her down, then walking her again and finally attending to her feet before putting her into a stall where a feed awaited her, Roz was aware of a decision—or at least the need to make a decision growing within her.

She watched the filly tuck into the feed bin hooked on to her half stable door and played with her forelock for a time, then wandered away to a secluded spot where she could see the track and the horses working undisturbed.

She found herself thinking that she had unwittingly got on to shaky ground. And that the crux of it all seemed to be that she had been deluding herself. She'd *thought* she had hidden her inner torment from Adam; she'd thought, well, I sleep with him whenever he wants it, I don't make a fuss, and if I hate myself afterwards that's my business ...

Yes, I did think that, she marvelled, and never even considered that he might know me so well. But why should I be so surprised? He certainly knew what would make me marry him. No, that puts him in the wrong light, it wasn't like that really, if I'm honest.

She plucked a stem of grass and chewed it with eyes narrowed as she tried to concentrate and to wonder a little desolately where she'd gone wrong, *why* she'd gone wrong, why her best intentions had misfired ...

She shrugged and watched two horses working together, pounding down the straight, then she closed her eyes and sniffed the air and simply listened for a while, to all the sounds that made up the life of a racing stable, the faint cracking of whips as the two horses on the track reached the winning posts, the clatter of hooves on concrete, horses snorting indignantly, soft voices, hoses gushing, buckets clanking. And there were the smells—molasses, manure, the smell of straw and tar, dust and grass, leather.

Adam Milroy had acquired his wealth in a variety of ways—he was good at wheeler-dealing, he had once told Roz. In fact, she'd learned that when he was a child, two things had fascinated him—electronics and horses, both of which he had acquired considerable understanding of. But it was his flair for computers that had seen the mushrooming of his small electronics business—started on a shoestring, Flavia always boasted—to a nationwide company.

And that, for a boy from the bush, Flavia always added, is really something. But Roz now knew that the 'bushie' tag was somewhat overdone. Werrington might have been an outback cattle property, but the Milroys had always contrived, through good times and bad, to send their children away to good schools, whatever else they might have gone without. And they had placed great store on not only education but culture, particularly Charles Milroy, who had read aloud to them every evening and conducted his own classes on a wide variety of subjects whenever he could lay his hands on his flock. He should have been a teacher, not a grazier, Margaret had told Roz once. He was mad about literature and music. So was her mother, and it became quite a battle of wits to evade their little sessions. 'Oddly enough,' said Margaret, 'Aunt Elspeth used to help us. She thought it was a lot of nonsense. Very down-to-earth and practical is our Aunt Elspeth. I think that's where Adam got his streak of practicality—it certainly wasn't from his father. Uncle Charles was a real dreamer.'

What about his mother? Roz had asked, and Margaret had thought for a bit, then shrugged and agreed that Aunt Flavia was actually quite a practical person too, yet in a different way from Aunt Elspeth, whose motto in life could be summed up in two words—no frills.

But it was his success in the electronics world that had allowed Adam to indulge his other passion, horses, although by the time he had grown up it could be said, and had been sometimes, that he had three great interests in life—beautiful women being the third.

Yet, while he made a profit on his breeding and racing involvements—Roz found it unthinkable that anything would mean so much to Adam that he would be prepared to lose money at it, and was oddly comforted by this thought—he had never raced or bred a champion. Certainly, some handy horses, quite a lot of them, but not one you could call an out-and-out champion.

And that's where I came in, she thought very early in the morning after her birthday party as she sat beside Adam's training track and his private training establishment with the sound of the voice of his private trainer ringing in her ears as some unfortunate strapper copped a mouthful over some misdemeanour.

'Life's really odd sometimes,' she said softly to herself. 'If Grandad hadn't... well, it all goes back a bit further, if my parents hadn't died and left me to my grandfather to be brought up, who was such a honey but a compulsive gambler... If *he* hadn't acquired Nimmitabel's dam Amanda Belle and got her in foal in extraordinary circumstances to a top-flight stallion... If our stables hadn't been burnt down, causing Grandad's death, and leaving me with an orphan foal, a mortgage, so many debts—well, I wouldn't be here today, would I?'

No, she thought, I wouldn't. But I am. I turned my back on Mike, I weighed up all the odds and came to a decision... what else can I do but stick to it?

'You were up very early, Roz.'

'Yes, I was, Adam,' she said patiently as she poured herself some coffee in the breakfast room. It was Saturday, she remembered, but although it was still early, Adam was already dressed for the races in a navy blue suit and a pink shirt with a white collar—although his jacket and blue tie were hung over the back of his chair. She was just about to comment on how early he was ready when he remarked,

'You said that with a curious air of resignation, Roz.'

'Did I?' She blinked and cast her mind back. 'Oh, um... maybe because you're the third person to mention it to me. Both Milly and Jeanette have just remarked on it. Fourth—Les was surprised too.'

'I see.' He held her gaze levelly and she wondered if there was something wrong with her appearance—she wore blue jeans, boots and a yellow and blue checked shirt and had tied her hair back loosely with a ribbon. But then he turned his attention back to his breakfast and said, reaching for the butter, 'So you were not trying to humour me?'

'Humour you?'

'Like a good little wife? If you recall we . . . er . . . had words last night.' He looked up briefly, his eyes glinting.

Roz swallowed a very hot mouthful of coffee and spluttered slightly. 'I recall,' she said when she was able to.

'Or perhaps you're waiting for me to humour you, Roz?' he said politely, and started to eat.

She watched and battled a tide of helplessness, wondering what had ever made her think she was a match for Adam Milroy in any way, but particularly in this dangerous mood. Yet only a short while ago she had made a decision to try and get their relationship back on its old footing, after fruitlessly pondering why she had allowed it to slip out of gear, so to speak, why she had allowed herself to be trapped into displaying such emotion. The only answer she had been able to come up with was that Jeanette's words the night before had somehow triggered everything that had happened since.

And she wondered, as she watched him eat his breakfast with the kind of precision he did most things, whether he still expected an answer from her.

Then his lashes lifted abruptly and he said, 'Well?'

She looked away and said barely audibly, 'No. I wasn't waiting for that.'

'I take it you didn't sleep very well last night.'

Roz licked her lips and looked back at him, her deep blue eyes shadowed themselves apart from the tell-tale faintly blue shadows beneath them, and a little spurt of bravado overcame her. 'Did you?'

Their gazes locked and held. 'No,' Adam said at last, then, 'Roz, if you're picturing yourself as barren, infertile or whatever you like to call it, you could be quite wrong. The reason you haven't become pregnant yet might be something as simple as extreme tension—no, don't look like that. It is a possibility.'

'I know, the doctor mentioned that, but two years,' she shrugged, 'seems a long time, and I wasn't always . . .' She stopped and bit her lip.

He studied her. 'If you could forget all about it, it might help.'

'Oh, Adam,' she sighed wearily, 'it's easy for you to say that and I do try not to dwell on it but . . .' She stopped and took a breath, thinking suddenly, this is the opening I need. 'Actually I wanted to talk to you about that—well, what happened last night, the things I said and so on. I don't——' she paused and trembled inwardly but forced herself to go on, 'I don't really know why it all boiled up like that, but maybe,' she tried to smile, 'it was for the best. Perhaps I got it all out of my system, and anyway, you knew it was there bothering me, didn't you? You said . . .' She broke off awkwardly.

Adam reached for the coffee pot. 'Go on.'

She winced inwardly, then said huskily, 'Now that I've realised how foolish I've been, I think I can change. I promise I won't . . . well, I've thought about it a lot this morning and to hate myself for . . .' She coloured and dried up.

'Hate yourself for enjoying being made love to?' he offered.

'Yes,' she whispered. 'That's ridiculous, isn't it?'

He smiled briefly. 'Not really. Not in our situation. But I've had a better idea,' he added as she looked at him confusedly. 'I thought it might be wise if we had a break from each other.'

Roz's lips parted and her eyes widened.

He waited for a moment, then started to speak, but she broke in, 'You mean—go away from each other?'

He studied her probingly, then he said, 'Not precisely. But I've got an extremely busy few months coming up, so I'll be away from home quite a lot and . . .'

'You mean—not sleep with each other? Because you're still angry with me? Is that . . .'

'Roz, no, not because of that. I'm not angry with you about anything. But,' his dark eyes narrowed as they rested on her pale face, 'perhaps we need time to stand back a bit from each other. Also, you'll be able to relax and stop worrying about whether you're getting pregnant.'

'How . . .' her voice seemed to stick in her throat, 'how many months?'

He shrugged. 'We don't have to be too specific, do we?'

'But how will you . . .?' She blushed vividly and closed her eyes, but her lashes flew up as she heard him laughing softly and she said indignantly and reproachfully, 'I was only . . .'

'Expressing very wifely concern?' he said with a grin. 'Don't worry, I plan to be *very* busy!'

She stared at him helplessly, totally taken aback by this turn of events, and yet if he'd suggested it last night she might have jumped for joy, mightn't she? And *wouldn't* it be a relief not to have to worry about getting pregnant, just for a little while? Only ...

'I don't know what to say. Do I have a choice?'

'Not while you're looking like this, no.'

'How am I looking?' she asked bewilderedly.

'Haunted,' he said briefly.

'I ... I ... I'm fine really,' she stammered.

'Well, perhaps this will make you finer,' he said, and she thought she detected a note of dryness in his voice, but he went on normally, 'Also, you have Nicky coming to stay for a while from Tuesday, isn't it? And then there's Nimmitabel. Les reckons she'll be ready for her first start fairly soon, so you have an exciting time ahead of you.'

'Yes. Yes,' Roz said dazedly. 'You won't miss that, will you?'

'No. Roz——' he hesitated, 'about Michael Howard, I'm sorry I broke the news to you like that. I'm not so old that I can't remember how traumatic one's first love affair can be.'

She blinked. 'It wasn't an affair! I mean, we didn't ...'

'I know. You proved that yourself, but all the same——' He shrugged.

Roz looked away. Then she asked, 'Was your first marriage your first love affair, Adam?'

'Not quite. But there was plenty of trauma there.' He smiled faintly. 'I told you that Louise left me for someone older,' he stood up, 'no doubt wiser but particularly, wealthier. Not that it was hard to be wealthier than I was in those days, but he was rather rich.'

'And now?' Roz asked.

He looked at her. 'Now what?'

'Is he still wealthier?'

'Not . . .' he stopped and looked rueful.

'Not any longer?'

'Not at the last count. But I stopped counting a few years back. He might have made a recovery. Roz . . .'

'Where are you going?'

'To work.'

'But it's Saturday. I thought you'd be going to the races—I thought we'd be . . . going to the races.'

Adam looked down at her for what seemed a very long time. Then he came over to her and sat on the edge of the table and picked up her hand. 'You can't,' he said, looking down at her slim fingers and his ruby engagement ring, 'stay awake for ever, my dear. Nor can you rely on me to help you to sleep for ever. You can do it on your own.'

'So it's to start now?' she said, and her lips trembled.

'Yes, Roz. I'm freeing you of all obligations for the time being. You know, I also know what it's like to be unable to relax, to be able to forget when everything seems to stand up and scream your memories to you. Not that mine were quite on the same scale as yours, not so . . . horrific. But we have one thing in common—what happened when I lost Werrington and you lost your grandfather was not our fault. It happened, that's all.'

'Yes,' she whispered, 'I guess so.'

'And the fact that you've been awake for nearly the last twenty-four hours can't change it.'

'No, but . . .'

'I know, I haven't helped exactly. But that's all the more reason for us to do this. You have to learn to relax, and this is the best way.'

Roz wandered upstairs into her bedroom after she had watched Adam drive away. She stared into her mirror and tried to see how she looked haunted. But all she could detect was that she looked dazed and tired—and apprehensive. Did that all add up to looking haunted? Certainly like a player who had lost the script...

She sighed and went through to her bathroom to have a shower, and afterwards she pulled on her favourite grey silk wrapper with birds of paradise on it and lay down on the bed to think. But to her immense surprise, when she woke up, she had fallen asleep and slept deeply and dreamlessly for hours.

To find, when she got up, her sister-in-law Nicky on the doorstep full of apologies because she had arrived a few days early, but she was broke, she said. Positively destitute, which she would hate to have to admit to her mother, which she'd thought of admitting to Adam last night but had not been able to nerve herself to, and the only other thing she had been able to come up with was to arrive early and sweat out the few days until her next allowance, availing herself of his hospitality at the same time—what did Roz think?

Roz didn't get a chance to say, because Nicky charged on—was that a coward's way out, not to mention really creepy, but didn't Roz share her sentiments that one small mouth to feed for an extra couple of days, especially one's sister's small mouth...?

'Nicky,' Roz broke in laughingly, 'come in, and think no more about it. Of course he won't mind. Anyway, we won't tell him if you'd rather not, and I'm thrilled you've come a couple of days early. How were the exams? I meant to ask you last night but forgot.'

'Horrific,' Nicky replied, rolling her dark eyes. 'Really hard, so I've got that on my conscience too. If I fail...'

'You won't,' said Roz confidently. 'You never have yet.'

'Yes, but I've been—well, not quite so conscientious this semester... I say, Roz, are there any other members of the family lurking around? Like Aunt Margaret or Mum or—God forbid!—Lucia?'

'Not a one, and none invited,' Roz assured her. 'Why?'

Nicky sighed with relief, then said comically out of the corner of her mouth, 'You ain't got no idea what it's like to have a large interfering family, kiddo, and especially one like the Milroys. Oh,' she stopped and coloured, 'well, you do now, but you've got Adam to use as a buffer, and to have *no* family mightn't be very nice, although I can't see it at present, but... oh damn, do you know what I mean, Roz?'

'Entirely,' said Roz with a grin. 'But if you're being harassed by the family at present—although I can't think why, because they all adore you, I'm sure Adam would be happy to act as a buffer for you too. He... seems to know how to handle them,' she added wryly.

But to her surprise, Nicola's face fell, and she sighed confusedly. 'If only I knew where Adam *stood*!'

'Nicky,' Roz said slowly, 'you're not thinking of shaving your head and going to join the Hare Krishnas or something like that, are you? Because...'

But Nicola started to laugh delightedly and said finally, 'Oh *God*, can you imagine it? Oh Roz, I'll remember that!'

'Nicky!' Roz exclaimed in some alarm.

And Nicola looked at her contritely, then kissed her on

the cheek. 'It's nothing,' she said gaily. 'Well, only that I am nineteen and I resent everyone trying to tell me how to run my life as if I was fifteen or sixteen still. I guess that's one of the penalties of being the baby of the family, though. Now, would it be too much to ask for a bite to eat? It's nearly lunchtime and I didn't have any breakfast, and ...'

'Come right this way,' Roz invited. But as they sat down to an informal lunch with Milly and Jeanette, both great fans of Nicky, Roz wondered if there was something more than the weight of family interest bothering her pretty, vibrant sister-in-law. And she found herself remembering again what Margaret had said, and discovered that there was something else niggling at the back of her mind to do with Nicky, only she couldn't dig it out.

Then she thought, we've got two weeks together, she might tell me of her own accord. If there *is* anything else to tell.

'By the way,' said Nicky that evening when they were watching a video in the den and laughing immoderately at the antics of Dudley Moore while they ate their supper off plates balanced on their knees, 'where *is* Adam? I thought it was Saturday today.'

'It is.' Roz licked her fingers.

'No races?'

'Oh yes, but he's working.'

Nicky raised her eyebrows. 'Working? Darling Roz, don't tell me we're going poor again!'

'Why do you say that?'

'Because—well, I didn't know he worked on Saturdays,' Nicky explained, looking nonplussed. 'You usually go the races, don't you? To tell the truth, I didn't expect to find you home when I arrived. I thought I might be able to sneak in.'

Roz started to speak, then paused as she was suddenly consumed by the enormity of having to explain that although Adam had never worked on a Saturday before during their entire marriage, that was what he was doing today, or had *said* that was what ...

But then she heard his tread outside the den and she looked around at the door and closed her eyes in silent ... relief? yes, when he walked in on them.

Nicky sprang up. 'Adam! You must be a mind-reader! We were just talking about you.'

'No wonder my ears were tingling!' Adam said with a grin, but his eyes sought Roz's over Nicky's shoulder as he hugged her.

And she found herself smiling with ... yes, relief again. Only a moment later Nicky unwittingly demolished it. 'Roz said you were working,' she confided artlessly, 'but I couldn't believe that, because according to Mum you don't need to work *ever* again. That's what she says anyway.' She struck a pose. 'My son Adam ...'

'I was, Nicky,' Adam interrupted, 'and of course I need to. Things don't run themselves, nor have I tapped the rainbow. But to what,' he enquired, 'do we owe the honour of your presence two days early? I thought your weekend was accounted for—oh, don't tell me! You're broke.'

Fortunately his perspicacity caused Nicky to blush brightly, then dissolve into rueful laughter—and to forget about the oddity of her beloved, kindest, most understanding brother working on a Saturday.

But Roz couldn't forget it, she found.

'How are you?' queried Adam, pouring himself a drink. Nicky had left them alone.

'Fine! Would you like some dinner? I'm sure there's some left, or I could make you something.'

'No, thanks, I've eaten.' He pulled his tie off and opened the white collar of his pink shirt, then took his drink over to the window while Roz rewound the video and turned the television off. In the ensuing silence she glanced across the room at him, standing tall and still with his back to her, apparently absorbed in the view although it was dark outside. She found herself marvelling because the last twenty-four hours—well, a bit longer, but not much—had again seen a radical change in her life, but like an iceberg, the largest part of it was below the surface. But then a lot of their life together had been like that, hadn't it? And like an iceberg, that was the tricky, dangerous bit. Why dangerous? she mused. Am I being imaginative?

Then she said quickly, 'I slept,' as he turned and caught her watching him. 'For hours.' But immediately she wondered if it was a diplomatic thing to have said. Wasn't it admitting that he was right?

But he only said, 'Good,' and came over to sit down in one of the comfortable leather armchairs, and when she sat down opposite him, he added, 'Would *you* like a drink, by the way? Now you're twenty-one.'

'No, thanks,' Roz said wryly. 'You were right about that gin last night. I didn't like it. So I think I'll stick to wine with meals and the odd aperitif.' She smoothed the skirt of her long aquamarine skirt which she wore with a navy blue peasant-style blouse with puffed sleeves, and aqua ribbon tying back her hair and navy blue flat velvet shoes.

'I like that outfit,' Adam remarked presently when she couldn't think of anything to say—well, how to express herself anyway.

Which was probably why she took his remark up so eagerly. 'Do you? Actually I chose it myself—Jeanette let me loose—but I think she approved. She said it was perfect for——' Roz stopped, then shrugged and smiled faintly, 'a lady of the manor to be comfortably at home in the evenings in. Jeanette has some ... rather old-fashioned notions, but then she's very wise too and ...'

'Well, I think she's right about everything on this occasion,' he broke in with his dark eyes looking amused. 'You are the lady of the manor,' he added.

Only in name at the moment, Roz thought but did not say.

But he went on, 'Do you always take Jeanette shopping with you?'

'Nearly always. Even your mother thinks she has a marvellous eye for clothes. Adam, do you think we could do something about that? I mean, put her through a dress designing course and a millinery course? Do you remember that hat I wore to the Prime Minister's Cup? Oh, well, you probably don't,' she shrugged as he narrowed his eyes, 'but ...'

'Yes, I do. You were all in sapphire blue that day, that made your eyes look like sapphires, except for the hat—I mean it wasn't all blue, it had pink rosebuds on it. It was very pert and attractive.'

Roz blinked. 'Oh. Well,' she said almost as if she'd forgotten what she'd been saying.

'Jeanette had something to do with the hat, I gather,' Adam suggested.

'Yes! She virtually remodelled it!' Roz said gratefully.

'It had this long yellow feather on it originally, but when we got it home, we decided we'd made an awful mistake because it made me look like ... something out of the Folies Bergère.'

Adam's teeth glinted in a smile. 'I can't imagine that.'

'Well, no, knowing the rest of me I don't suppose you can,' she said, smiling back with an imp of mischief dancing in her eyes suddenly. 'But the point is ...'

'Jeanette replaced the feathers with the rosebuds?'

'She *made* them. She stiffened some silk in beaten egg white and before it had set she fashioned these gorgeous lifelike rosebuds out of it. Then she sprayed them with hair spray in case I was beset by wasps—she learnt that trick from her mother, who decorated a Christmas cake with stiffened ribbon, but the ants got to it.'

'Perhaps the icing enticed the ants,' Adam said gravely.

'Perhaps,' Roz conceded. 'I didn't have any trouble with creepy-crawlies, but ...'

'As for the rest of you,' he interrupted, 'I think they'd have adored you at the Folies Bergère, but I doubt if you'd have liked it much. That's what I meant.'

'I ... wouldn't have thought I was ... buxom enough for that kind of thing. What a horrible word, but do you know what I mean?' And she was assailed by a fit of very natural laughter.

Adam laughed too, then he said, 'It's not always a question of being buxom, Roz. Your figure's perfect, for you. In fact it's astonishingly lovely.'

Her smile faded. 'Then why——?' she whispered. 'I mean, if you think that why are we ...' She stopped and twisted her hands together uncomfortably.

He sat up. 'I thought you'd understood and accepted it.'

'I . . .'

'Roz, moments ago you were happy and relaxed and you were chatting to me as you haven't for ages. You slept today, and I've never known you to sleep *during* the day—don't you see, it's working already, my dear.'

'I can see,' she cleared her throat, 'that I haven't been a very successful wife, which I promised myself I would be, you know. I didn't say to myself, well, I haven't got much option about this, so I'll make it as difficult as possible. I said the opposite. I . . . want you to know that, Adam.' She looked down at her hands, then lifted her lashes.

'Do you think I don't?' he retorted.

She flinched. 'Then . . .'

'Roz,' the light of impatience died out of his eyes suddenly, 'look, all I'm suggesting is a short break from each other, that's all, and I want to make sure you understand that before I go. It's nothing to get into a panic about.'

'Go?' Her eyes widened.

'To Japan,' he said wearily. 'Just for a week on business. I told you this morning that I had a busy time ahead—well, it's all to do with the opportunity to acquire the agency for a very sophisticated Japanese electronic sound system, with the distribution rights, etcetera. I decided today that my best bet was to go over in person, so I'm flying out tomorrow. But you'll have Nicky and . . .'

'I know,' Roz cut in dryly, and a little spark lit her blue eyes, but she looked away quickly, unwilling for him to see that she was curiously angry suddenly, and not only because he had made it sound as if she needed a whole host of minders. Then she forced herself to breathe deeply, although in a sense she was happy to be angry because at least she didn't feel quite so foolish and it seemed to keep other, more complex emotions at bay.

'I hope you're taking over a plentiful supply of stuffed koala bears,' she told him. 'They love them in Japan. I was reading only the other day about a Japanese tourist who bought fourteen, dropped them in the Brisbane River—accidentally, of course—and rushed back to buy another fourteen.' She even managed to smile as she delivered this thrilling bit of information, which might have been lodged at the back of her mind for just this moment! she thought.

Adam looked at her steadily, then grimaced and said, 'I'll certainly take your advice, ma'am. I wonder if they sell them at the airport.'

CHAPTER THREE

'ISN'T this just bliss!' Nicky exclaimed enthusiastically as she rearranged herself on her lounger beside the pool.

It was a clear hot day with the lovely smell of summer in the air and the pool sparkled beside them, sprinklers netted the lawn further away with diamond drops of water, and to cap off the bliss, Nimmitabel had recorded an extremely fast track gallop earlier that morning.

'Mmm,' Roz agreed, but in fact she wasn't thinking of their day but whether it was snowing in Tokyo.

'Roz, were you ever in love before you met Adam? I mean, was he your first love?'

The warning bell that sounded in Roz's brain effectively banished images of winter in the Land of the Rising Sun. She sat up and reached for some suntan lotion to smooth over her ivory skin, rather exposed today in a scarlet bikini, and cautioned herself to think carefully about what she said. Had someone divined the real nature of her marriage to Adam?

'Um . . . I did *think* I was in love with someone before I met Adam, but . . .'

'Oh, do tell me!' Nicky sat up and crossed her legs, looking at Roz expectantly. 'What was he like?'

'He was the boy next door,' Roz said rather ruefully. 'We more or less grew up together, and because I didn't have a mother, his mother was really good to me. And we started out being brotherly and sisterly to each other, but one day it . . . changed. Much to some people's dismay,' she added slowly.

'Who?' asked Nicky avidly.

'His father mostly—well, his mother too.'

'But why?'

Roz hesitated. 'We *were* very young and . . . perhaps they were afraid I'd inherited some of the less stable facets of my grandfather's character. He was rather hopeless with money, you see. As soon as it came his way he gambled it on horses or dogs.'

'Then how come you inherited such a fabulous filly? I mean, on her breeding alone, if she breaks down tomorrow, which God forbid—but . . .'

'Nicky!' Roz exclaimed.

'Sorry. Shouldn't have even cherished the notion,' Nicky said hastily, and added, 'She certainly looks as sound as a bell, but her potential as a brood mare *is* enormous, with her bloodlines. Isn't that one of Adam's pet theories?' She smiled suddenly. 'If you'd been anyone else he might have married you just to get his hands on your horse . . . have I said something wrong?'

Roz disclaimed hurriedly.

'Oh, good,' Nicky said cheerfully. 'I just thought you looked a bit odd all of a sudden. But to get back to the point—if you had such a spendthrift grandfather and no other background to speak of . . .' She blushed and pulled a face of extreme embarrassment.

So much so that Roz had to laugh, and at the same time experience a feeling of relief that the drift of the conversation had altered.

'Actually, your background has always been a bit of a mystery, Roz,' Nicky added apologetically. 'I mean, you could have knocked us all down with a feather when Milly broke the news about the marriage. We'd never even heard of you or known that he'd met you. It must have been love at first sight ...' she sighed.

'Oh, there's no mystery,' said Roz, sensing danger again, and she added, 'Adam knew my grandfather—he was a horse trainer, you see, and—well, it all came about over horses, Nimmitabel particularly, but her background is much more interesting than mine. It's like a fairy tale, and anyway, I guess it is my background too.'

'Oh good, I love a fairy story!'

So Roz embarked with relief on the story of how Nimmitabel's dam, a champion race mare, had contracted a mystery virus and eventually been judged infertile as a result of it and finally sold at a dispersal sale as a hack when her owner had died. That was when Roz's grandfather had been possessed of a quixotic impulse and bought her out of sentiment, remembering his wins on her, no doubt. He always remembered his wins but rarely his losses. And he'd brought her home to their Beenleigh property which was already overflowing with horses, most of them broken down, that he was trying to patch up to get to the races.

'Oh my,' he had said to Roz with tears in his eyes, 'she was a bonny sight streaming past the winning post. It's a terrible shame she can't be bred from. But that's life.'

Roz had enquired what they would do with her.

'We're going to treat her like the lady, the grand lady she is,' he had replied, and so they had.

'She was beautiful too,' said Roz with a sigh. 'Very gentle, but every inch an aristocrat.'

'But if Amanda Belle—even I've heard of her racing

deeds—was infertile how on earth did she have Nimmitabel?'

'Well, there's no doubt they tried desperately to get her in foal for about seven seasons in a row and possibly might have kept on trying if her owner hadn't died and his estate been all sold. But seven years is a long time to persevere with a mare, and it must have looked hopeless, and *we* could only assume that time had finally healed the problem. But it came quite out of the blue to us. We didn't even suspect she was in season when the drama occurred.'

'So you didn't send her to Kosciusko?'

'No! We could never have afforded it even if we'd known she could conceive. What happened was that he was being floated to a new stud when the transport broke down virtually right outside our gates. And they had to take him off because he was kicking the truck to pieces and dreadfully stirred up, but that proved to be a mistake, because they just couldn't handle him.'

Nicky said, 'Ah! I begin to see.'

'Yes,' Roz agreed wryly. 'He broke his headstall, somehow got rid of the rearing bit and took off up our drive, which, as you can imagine, caused a major panic, because he's worth a fortune.'

'And you saw all this?'

'Oh yes! One of the handlers had come up to the house to use the phone before Kosciusko broke loose. In fact there was quite a band of spectators. Michael—he was the boy next door—and his father and, fortunately as it turned out, the local policeman, although he'd come to see Grandad about a cow we had that had strayed. But to cut a long story short, Kosciusko found Amanda Belle in her paddock, broke through the fence to get to her, and when we all arrived, faint but pursuing, he was covering her.'

'My God, how wonderfully romantic!' exclaimed Nicky, her dark eyes glowing.

'Well, it was and it wasn't,' said Roz. 'Everyone was furious—at least his handlers were—and petrified he'd hurt himself and I suppose had visions of losing their jobs. And Grandad was livid about his precious Amanda Belle being treated so cavalierly ...' She broke off to smile. 'He kept saying—my God, is that any way to treat a lady! If he's hurt her!'

'Had he?'

'No, but the biggest miracle was he hadn't hurt himself apart from some cuts and scratches. And after it was all over he allowed himself to be caught like a lamb. That was when everyone repaired to the house for a stiff drink.' Roz paused. 'And that was when Grandad surprised the life out of us all,' she said reminiscently.

'Go on,' said Nicky after a time.

'Well,' Roz shrugged, 'he insisted that the incident had to be recorded and reported. Not, he said to the handlers, because he wanted to lose them their jobs, in fact he'd go out of his way to corroborate that it had all been an unavoidable accident, but he said it had to be recorded that Kosciusko had served Amanda Belle in front of quite a few witnesses. Naturally they all recognised her name and were doubly upset when they remembered she was incapable of being got in foal. But he just kept saying, you never know, you never know ... And the policeman agreed with him, so they didn't have much choice.

'I can remember thinking it was all a waste of time, but he was adamant, and he said afterwards that he'd just had this curious premonition during that tempestuous mating. The rest is history. Eleven months later Amanda Belle gave birth to Nimmitabel, although she died, and . . . Grandad died the night before.'

'Tell me,' Nicky said softly.

Roz stared unseeingly towards the sprinklers. 'Our stables burnt down. Someone on a neighbouring property had started a grass fire, but the wind changed and before we even knew it was lit it was roaring towards our place and the stables were directly in its path. You've no idea how quickly a fire can move. We just didn't have time to get all the horses out, but Grandad rescued Amanda Belle, then went back. He . . . he loved horses and he couldn't stand hearing them. It was the smoke that got him. But his last words to me were—whatever you do, look after her and her foal, because it's going to be a champion,' she said huskily. 'He was quite convinced of that from the moment he knew the miracle *had* happened and she was in foal to Kosciusko.'

'Oh, Roz, how awful!' Nicky said softly. 'I'm sorry I made you remember. You must have *nightmares* about it.'

'Sometimes,' Roz admitted. 'But . . . well, it helps to think he might have been right. Not that you can really tell until they race, but . . .' She shrugged.

'Well, at least you met Adam then,' Nicky reflected, and dabbed away a tear.

'I had met him once before,' Roz told her. 'When I was fourteen or fifteen, but the second time—well . . .'

'You fell in love? How marvellous!'

'Yes. Yes, it was.'

'And you were *still* very young,' Nicky said enthusiastically.

Roz glanced at her, but Nicky went on, 'It's really funny, you know, Roz—I've known you for two years now but hardly know anything about you, which makes me feel rather guilty, but Mum was mostly responsible for that.'

'Oh?' Roz raised her eyebrows.

'Yes. In case you hadn't realised, Mum adores Adam, but although you came as such a surprise, I think she must have approved of you almost straight away, because she warned us all off. I mean, she told us she didn't want you to feel as if you were facing the Spanish Inquisition—which wasn't precisely how she treated Louise, believe me, although I liked her, but probably the least said soonest mended about *that*. But it's led to the curious situation of none of us knowing you very well—I feel I didn't anyway until today. I'm so glad that's changed now,' Nicky finished warmly.

Roz sniffed and blinked. 'So am I. Sorry . . .'

'Oh, Roz,' Nicky said softly, 'you didn't think we didn't like you? It wasn't that!'

'No, I know—well, I hoped so. Oh, there's Milly calling us for lunch. I hope you're hungry, because she thinks you're looking thin and plans to compensate, I suspect.'

It was over lunch that Jeanette mentioned she'd had a phone call from her mother to let her know that her elder sister had been safely delivered of a baby girl, her third child in four years but her first daughter. Roz immediately thought she detected a faintly wistful gleam in Jeanette's eyes, and after consulting Milly, she suggested that Jeanette take a week off so she could visit her sister and help out with the rest of the family. Jeanette resisted for a time, but in the end was no match for both Milly and Roz.

'You're sure you'll be all right without me?' were her last words.

'Quite sure,' Roz said gravely but with an inward smile and a feeling of affection, and found herself reflecting that while she might not be pleasing Adam currently, his family and his staff appeared to be another matter. And she thought of the tears that had come with Nicky's revelations earlier and the corresponding discovery of how much it meant to her to have the family's approval.

Several things happened that evening.

Adam rang from Tokyo, and Richard and Amy and Angelo arrived to spend the evening.

'Hang on—can you hang on a moment?' Roz said breathlessly into the phone. 'I'll take this in your study. There's too much noise here.'

'Hello?' she said moments later. 'Adam?'

'I'm here, Roz. You were right about the noise. Having a party?'

'No! At least, I'm not, but Angelo and Amy and Richard have come to see Nicky and spend the evening, so it's become rather like a party.'

He laughed down the line. 'I can imagine! But you don't have to sound guilty.'

'I'm not,' she said quickly. 'How are you?'

'Exhausted, to tell the truth. I've been on the go since

the moment I arrived.'

'Have you got the agency, do you think?'

'Yes, but it will take another few days to tie up all the loose ends. How are *you*?'

'Oh, congratulations,' said Roz sincerely. Then, 'I'm fine. Nicky and I are enjoying ourselves doing nothing much. Er . . . your mother's coming down tomorrow to spend the day with us and Margaret rang up earlier to say she might pop in this week. Oh, Adam, you should have seen Nimmitabel this morning! Les organised a jump-out with three other two-year-olds including the Mirror-dot colt, but she was just too good for them and the time was sensational!' She told him all the details.

'No sign of shin soreness?' he asked when she had finished.

'No. Les is watching her like a hawk.'

'Good.'

There was a short silence, then she asked him what time it was in Tokyo.

'An hour earlier than it is at Little Werrington.'

'Is it snowing?'

'No, but it's very cold. Why do you ask?'

'I just wondered,' she said softly. 'Are you doing anything this evening?'

'I think I'm about to be entertained in the time-honoured Japanese way.'

'Do you mean . . .?'

'Well, my hosts have been rather mysterious, but they did ask me if I'd ever seen a real geisha. By the way, Roz, before you imagine . . .'

'I'm not imagining anything like that,' she protested.

'I've read all about geishas, and their primary purpose is to entertain you.'

'Have you now?' remarked Adam after a moment.

'Yes, I have. I don't quite know how it works with foreigners, but I'm sure they're according you an honour. So don't fall asleep, even if you can't understand a word.'

'No, ma'am!' he said. 'I'll be on my best behaviour.'

Roz had to laugh and he laughed too. Then he said, 'There's someone at the door, so I guess my car has arrived. Sleep well.'

'You too. And keep warm. Goodbye.'

Back in the den Roz found it hard to keep up with the high spirits of the others, but not only that. She felt jittery and nervous, as if her equilibrium had been mysteriously disrupted, and finally excused herself, not without some difficulty.

'Roz! The night's young yet,' Nicky protested.

'I know, but . . .'

'Darling Roz, don't desert us!' This was Angelo. 'Or are you telling us politely to hoof it?'

'No! I'd love you to stay and enjoy yourselves, so please do. I'm just . . . tired.'

It was Richard who said gently, 'I think Roz might be missing Adam, folks, as well as being tired, so back off. Goodnight, Roz. Are you sure you don't mind us staying on?'

'No, really I don't,' she said to him gratefully, and thought how nice he was.

But once in her bedroom she was forced to acknowledge the truth of his words. She *was* missing Adam, but it was worse. She was desperately trying not to think of him in the arms of some exquisitely beautiful accomplished geisha . . .

She put her hand over her mouth and blinked several times to stem tears of . . . what? Loneliness? Fright. *Jealousy* . . .?

'Oh God,' she whispered, and chewed at the tip of her forefinger, 'have I been . . . very blind? Not known what was happening to me. Have I been tilting at windmills? How *did* this happen to me? Perhaps I have to go back to the beginning, that awful day two weeks after the fire . . .'

She had lived with her grandfather in his old-fashioned Queensland colonial house since she was ten. It was a wooden, rambling house with verandas all round, set on twenty acres west of Beenleigh, which laid claims to being a satellite suburb of Brisbane, but in those days, the days during which Roz had grown up, had escaped being a suburb of anything, just a backwater off the Pacific Highway between Brisbane and the Gold Coast. And they had been far enough out of town to qualify for being country anyway.

She'd grown up surrounded by horses, an eccentric grandfather who had cared for her greatly and imbued her not only with his love of horses but a curiosity about most things. And while his erratic gambling habits had ensured that they were never affluent except in short bursts, the old homestead was filled with beautiful, solid, very old furniture, faded but beautiful chintz coverings and hangings and a collection of copper and brassware that had been her grandmother's passion. There were also books by the dozen, a lot of them spotted with mildew and from another era, but by the time she was fifteen, Roz had been throughly conversant with Jeffery Farnol, Mikhail Sholokov, Dorothy Sayers, and Josephine Tey among others.

After the first shock of grief for her parents, she had grown into her grandfather's lifestyle amazingly well—she had always been the apple of his eye, he used to tease her. And as she'd grown up they had been friends as well as relations.

It had all ended in a blaze of orange flames and choking smoke, and the belated wail of a fire engine siren with an ambulance siren not far behind.

Two weeks to the day afterwards, a stranger had called on her, and what he had come to say had precipitated a lot of what had happened since. Roz remembered it all so clearly . . .

'I can't, and I don't see how you can make me.' Her voice rose shakily. 'Just go away and leave me alone!'

'Lady . . .'

'I'll ring the police if you come one step closer. I don't even know you from a bar of soap. As for handing over a foal to you, you must be out of your mind!'

The man across the kitchen from her appeared to hesitate and his close-set eyes flickered over her in a way that filled her with revulsion. He was in his late twenties, she judged, and strongly built, but if that and his horrible way of looking at her weren't bad enough, what he had come to tell her was.

He chose now to repeat it. 'Look, love,' he said, 'your grandpa owes me a lot of money. He bet with me on credit, see, and ran up quite a little account . . .'

'Why did you *let* him?' Roz broke in intensely, and received a mocking look in return.

'It's my business, honey. But,' he shrugged, 'recently it began to get out of hand. He wasn't settling even with his lack of usual promptness, so I spoke to him about it—leant on him a little,' he said softly, and paused as Roz shivered. He continued with a small, satisfied smile, 'That's when he told me not to worry, he had a fortune coming his way. I said, oh yeah? He said yes and told me about this horse he'd bred.'

'It's barely two weeks old!' Roz cried. 'He had no way of knowing it would survive the birth—the dam died. How *could* he?'

'Well, he did, love. But as a matter of fact I took that up with him too. I also asked him if he was planning to sell it as a foal. He said once people knew the breeding he'd have no trouble doing that, only he'd rather not. But if he didn't punt his way out of trouble, he'd sell a share in it, that's what he *said*. Only he punted his way deeper into trouble, that's what he *did*. Now,' Roz backed as he moved closer and towered over her, 'I agree there's a potential fortune in that foal. *Potential*, mind. If you know anything at all about horses you'll also know there's one hell of a lot can happen to them between the time they get born to the time they get to the races, if they ever do. But she's a filly, so . . .'

'But . . .'

'Let me finish, little lady,' the man said menacingly. 'I'm prepared to take that filly foal off your hands and in exchange, wipe out all your grandpa's debts—in fact I reckon it's the least you owe me, because in a sense, he was using her as collateral to bet with me, see what I mean? I also reckon it's a generous offer on my part, because like I said, filly or not, anything could go wrong—she might even take half a lifetime to breed like her ma and I'd have nothing.'

'And ... and in the meantime, I'll have nothing,' Roz stammered.

'You got nothing now, lady,' he sneered. 'Apart from a mountain of debts. How do you think you're going to rear the foal anyway? It all costs money. At least this way you'll be relieved of some of your debts and you won't have a flaming horse to feed. So think about it,' he advised softly, then struck terror into Roz's heart by adding, 'only don't take too long, sweetheart. Because it seems to me you're a mighty desirable young lady and it might occur to me to up the ante—if you know what I mean.'

The way he looked her over again left Roz in no doubt as to his meaning, and she went white and stumbled back another step as the man loomed over her and put his arms out as if to take her into them.

'No!' she whispered frantically.

'I agree,' said a voice from behind them.

Roz's tormentor whipped round, obscuring her vision, and she saw the muscles of his shoulders bunch up beneath his thin shirt and then relax, but with an effort of will. Then he stepped aside and Roz gasped, because the very last person she expected to see was lounging in the doorway and watching them dispassionately—Adam Milroy.

He straightened and said casually, 'Menacing women and children might be up your street, Stan—I can't honestly say it surprises me—but it isn't up mine. So beat it, mate, and if I were you I wouldn't return.'

'Well, well,' drawled Stan Hawkins, 'I wonder what brings *you* to this neck of the woods, *Mr* Milroy? Let me guess.'

'Don't bother, Stan,' Adam advised, and moved aside. And although his words were mild enough there was something in his voice that sent a shiver down Roz's spine.

It seemed to have a similar effect on Stan Hawkins, because he started to bluster then about having legitimate business with Roz, but as those dark eyes held his mercilessly, he ran out of steam and finally picked up his jacket and stormed out.

Roz stayed as still as a statue until she heard his car drive away, then she moved precipitously and dashed out of the kitchen door just in time and to her despair was sick in the flower bed below the steps.

'I . . . I . . .' she whispered.

'It's all right,' Adam Milroy said prosaically. 'Why don't you go inside and have a wash while I find a spade.'

'But . . .'

'No buts. Actually,' he smiled at her, 'I'm quite used to this. I have a sister who gets car-sick, plane-sick—I suspect she could get sick on a bicycle if she put her heart and soul into it! Off you go.'

Roz hesitated painfully, then took his advice.

He must have found a spade pretty quickly because he was back in the kitchen before she was and he'd put the kettle on and some toast into the toaster.

'I . . .' she began.

'Sit down,' he ordered.

'I . . . I'll make it,' she said with an effort. 'I'd rather.'

Adam Milroy looked at her thoughtfully and then smiled, a battened-down version, but all the same . . . Then he sat down and said, 'I'm Adam, by the way, and I believe we've met, but it was years ago and I can't remember your name, though I've got the feeling it was something unusual.'

'Rozalinda . . . er . . . but everyone calls me Roz, with a z.'

He raised his dark eyebrows. 'I was right.'

'It was my father's idea. I don't know why.'

'Roz,' he said slowly.

The toast popped up and the kettle whistled and she didn't have to say anything more until she'd set out the tea things. In fact, when she tried to speak then, he motioned her to eat and drink first.

'Now,' he said at last, 'I didn't hear all of that unpleasant conversation, but I gather some disaster befell your grandfather?'

She told him, haltingly at first, and then like a rising tide that could not be stemmed it all came out—including her anguish that her grandfather, beloved as he had been, could have virtually gambled away Amanda Belle's precious foal.

'It's like a disease, my dear,' Adam Milroy said quietly.

'But he was so wonderful in every other way!'

'I know. So,' his dark gaze flickered over her, 'you've been left in dire straits, young Roz. How old are you?'

'Nineteen, nearly,' she said indistinctly as she swallowed the last of her tea. 'And I don't mind being left with nothing so much, but the thought of having to hand Nimmitabel over to that . . . that man . . .'

'Nimmitabel?' he interrupted. 'Oh, *I* get it. Mount Kosciusko, the Snowy Mountains, Nimmitabel which is in that area and also reflects Amanda Belle.' He smiled. 'Well chosen, but there's no question of you having to hand the foal over to Stan Hawkins.'

'Then why did he come?' Her blue eyes were round.

'Because he hoped to frighten you into doing just that, probably,' Adam Milroy said grimly. 'Although legally . . .' he shrugged. 'He could have had a crafty plan up his sleeve to backdate the transaction. What's the situation on this place?' He looked around.

'Mortgaged,' Roz said tearfully.

'And your grandfather had other debts apart from bookmakers?'

She nodded. 'The feed merchant, the vet . . .' She gestured helplessly.

'And he left it all to you?'

She said sadly, 'He didn't plan to die.'

'I know. I meant, are you his sole beneficiary?'

'Oh. Yes.'

'All right.' Adam Milroy drummed his fingers on the table, then said interrogatively, 'Do you know what happens now?'

Roz tried to think. 'There's been so much . . . I had to scour the countryside for a wet-nurse for the foal, the funeral, all the injured horses . . . But I've been in touch with the solicitor who has the will. I've an appointment with him and he said he'd explain it all to me.'

'I can tell you. Creditors of a . . . deceased person are entitled to make claims against their estate. Now if the claims exceed the cash available then the assets of the estate, if there are any, have to be put up for sale and the proceeds divided among the creditors. Stan Hawkins would have known all this, which is why, no doubt, he was so eager to get his hands on the foal beforehand.'

'Oh yes, I see,' Roz said slowly. 'So that means Nimmitabel will have to go up for action?'

'Yes, it does,' he said rather gently. 'I imagine, from what you've told me, she's about the estate's only unencumbered asset. I don't suppose she's in *your* name, by any chance?'

Roz shook her head. 'He was going to make me a partner in the foal, but . . .'

'Yes. Well, as to what price she would bring, that's rather hard to say. Kosciusko progeny don't come cheap and there's not been one yet, to my knowledge, that could top off the breeding of this foal. But there's also a lot hanging in the wind, as they say. The executor appointed in the will—and I presume there's one if the will has been properly drawn up—might well decide to . . . make other arrangements for the foal, because all these things take time.'

She flinched visibly and he looked at her keenly.

'You do have yourself to provide for, Roz. Do you have a job?'

She shook her head. 'Not really. I've been working part-time at a saddlery shop in Beenleigh, but it's closing down soon. Other than that I was Grandad's strapper. But I . . .' her voice shook, 'I'm sure I could find something else.'

He sat back and said sceptically, 'Perhaps. Don't you have any other relations?'

'No. Not close, anyway.'

'And did you never dream of doing anything else with

your life other than helping your grandfather with his horses and working part-time in a saddlery shop?'

Roz bit her lip at the rather sardonic note in his voice. Then she said quietly but steadily, 'Yes, I have. I've dreamt of travelling, learning more about so many things—art, music, cookery ... I'd like to be able to understand how the economy works and how computers work, and I'd love to really delve into old-fashioned herbal remedies. I'd like to be able to remove the threat of nuclear wars for ever and have lots of children. I *love* horses and I always will, but ...' She stopped and coloured, because he was looking at her with a curious intentness. 'I mean ...' She shrugged awkwardly.

'Don't look embarrassed. That was rather well said and I'm sorry if I sounded patronising.' He grimaced, then added, 'On top of it, you're unusually lovely, which has already caused you some problems.'

Roz flushed brightly this time. Not because his thoughtful gaze in any way resembled Stan Hawkins', rather it was the totally dispassionate sort of appraisal with which a good judge of horseflesh might sum up a yearling filly. But it did have something to do with that; while her looks didn't seem to particularly appeal to boys of her own age they did to older men—not, she amended to herself, that she could possibly attract Adam Milroy, but he had obviously discerned this curious fact. Of course Mike was different, Mike *knew* her.

But it had puzzled and disturbed her, and she had even discussed it with her grandfather, how no one at school apart from Mike had ever taken a great interest in her, whereas she was increasingly subject to the kind of looks from older men which made her hotly uncomfortable.

'It takes a bit of age and experience to recognise the kind of quality you have, Roz,' he had said slowly, and chewed his lip rather worriedly. 'Also when you're a bit shy—well, teenage boys are often great big shy hulks themselves and don't know how to handle it. That's why they go for the bolder ones. But don't you worry your head about it. You've got years before you need to.'

Not years, she thought ironically, now. And then the other factor to make me feel uncomfortable is that once upon a time, half a lifetime ago, or so it seems, I met Adam Milroy and ... had some rather dramatic daydreams about him.

She bit her lip and realised that the same Adam Milroy was sitting across the table from her, staring at her quizzically. 'I've got a boyfriend,' she said quickly.

He raised an eyebrow and looked amused, but said, 'Good. Where is he?'

'He lives next door. I've known him and his family for ages ...' She petered out nervously.

'Then,' Adam said consideringly, 'couldn't you stay with them for the time being?'

Roz stared down at her hands 'I was.'

'What went wrong?'

'Nothing! I ... they've gone to a wedding up country, one of Mrs Howard's nieces, but they'll be back tomorrow.'

'Do they ... approve of you and their son?' he asked after a moment.

She hesitated, then said with a sigh, 'I think they think we're too young to ... well ...'

'How old is this Mike?'

'Nineteen—we're nearly the same age. He's studying

commerce and has two years to go.'

There was silence, and it occurred to Roz that she had revealed her life history and nearly all her problems to a man she barely knew, who couldn't possibly be interested anyway, and she said stiffly, 'I'm sorry, I don't know why you came today, but I'm sure it wasn't to listen to my troubles. By the way, why did you come?'

'I met your grandfather at the races a couple of months ago. We've known each other for years on and off. I once bought a horse from him—that's why I was here last time. But anyway, he told me about the Amanda Belle miracle and invited me to come and see her. I'd have come sooner, but a trip overseas intervened. That's also why I didn't know about his death, I only got back the day before yesterday.'

'Oh . . .'

'How did she die? From the effects of the fire?'

'No, although she went into labour straight afterwards, but it was a haemorrhage. There was nothing we could do, it just,' she closed her eyes, 'was hopeless. She died with her head in my lap.'

Adam didn't try to offer any sympathy, but his silence was oddly comforting, and she asked tremulously after a time, 'Would you like to see the foal?'

'Very much'.

He was good with the foal and the old mare who had lost her own foal and was performing the services of wet-nurse.

'What do you think?' she asked.

He smiled slightly. 'She's a honey.'

Roz stroked the velvety nose and was playfully bunted in return. 'I hope she doesn't grow up with a split personality,' she said wryly. 'I had to try to bottle-feed her for a few days and she still seems to think I'm good for a meal!'

This was demonstrated when they finally left the paddock and the foal looked almost humanly undecided and forlorn, until the old mare whickered and she skittered towards it with relief.

Adam Milroy laughed and Roz said, 'See what I mean?'

He said nothing for a moment, then, 'I do,' soberly.

He left not long after that, commenting only on the fact that there seemed to be a storm on the way. Roz agreed a little worriedly, looking at the bank of boiling black clouds on the horizon because she had no stabling now for the mare and foal. And as she watched the beautiful maroon Jaguar drive away her mind was half on the possibility of converting the garage into a makeshift stall.

The speed with which the storm seemed to be approaching convinced her to do it rather than think about it, and she drove the utility out and parked it under the house, and was just struggling with a bale of straw to lay on the floor, when the maroon Jaguar drove up again.

She stared at it, but Adam Milroy wasted no words. 'I came back because I just heard on the car radio that there's a line of severe hailstorms headed this way that have wreaked havoc further inland.' He stopped and with a sharp glance took in the situation. 'Good idea,' he said briefly, and heaved the bale of straw off the back of the utility as if it was a packet of flour. 'I'll do this while you round them up.'

A door on the veranda slammed in the rising wind and

the afternoon was eerily dark now. Roz hesitated for only a bare moment before grabbing a headstall and lead and starting to run.

It was raining by the time she rounded up the old mare, who chose to be dithery, but when Adam loomed up he patted her neck briefly and thrust a hand through the headstall, skull-dragged her for a few paces until she decided she'd met her match and meekly and almost coyly followed him. Roz and the foal had to run to keep up.

When they reached the double garage doors, the mare again displayed some reluctance, but then sniffed the straw and was coaxed to go in, and Nimmitabel trotted in after her. Just as they closed the doors, the hail started.

'Oh, your car!' cried Roz above the growing cacophony on the old tin roof. 'Drive it under the house—I'll move some gear . . .'

Not many minutes later and not any too soon they were up in the safety of the house, soaked to the skin but safe from the wild, whirling world outside of white hailstones, many of them the size of golf balls.

Roz had seen hail before, but never like this—within minutes the landscape all around resembled a jagged snow scene. The noise was incredible as the deadly white missiles pounded down on the roof, and she shuddered to think of being caught outside in it, of the mare and foal out in it. Adam Milroy put his arm around her slim shoulders and she was intensely grateful to him for coming back, just for being there . . .

But it was ten minutes before she could say as much, before the hail passed and it was only rain drumming on the roof and they could make themselves heard. Then he only smiled and said it was the least he could have done. By which time it was almost too dark to see, so she went to put on a light, but nothing happened.

She looked helplessly at the switch and tried again, but again nothing happened. Adam Milroy remarked, 'It's not to be wondered at, there could be power lines down. Have you any alternative source of power?'

'The stove and the fridge are gas,' she told him, 'and I have some hurricane lamps. So I won't starve and I'll have some light—I'll be fine now, really I will, if you'd like to . . . I mean . . . I'm sure the worst is over and . . . She peered through the gloom at him.

But all he said was, 'Got a torch?'

'Oh yes, two, but . . .'

'Then I'll go down and check the horses. You get those hurricane lamps going in the meantime.'

'Well . . .' But perhaps, like the old mare, she sensed a will that was no match for her, because she went into the kitchen and got the torches and gave him one. While he was away, she used the other to dig out the lamps and prime them and light them. She was just wondering what was taking him so long, if the mare and foal had panicked at the noise and the unfamiliar confines and hurt themselves, when he came into the kitchen, looked around approvingly and said, 'I'm afraid you're going to have to put me up for the night, Roz. The reason you have no electricity is that the storm uprooted an old tree beside the gate—it brought the powerline down. It's also completly barred the driveway.'

She stared at him in the soft light with her lips parted and her eyes wide, until he raised an eyebrow and said with his lips twisting, 'Do you mind so very much? I'm sorry, there seems to be no help for it, but you don't have to worry that I'd take advantage of you.'

'No!' She rushed into speech. 'Oh no, I didn't ... that wasn't ... I just feel so terribly guilty ... I ...'

Adam looked ironically amused for a moment, then his gaze softened and he said, 'You're also very sweet, young Roz.'

It was a night Roz was to remember.

It rained all night, sometimes tempestuously, so that the house creaked rather alarmingly, but she could only feel safe and dry and with that awful sense of loneliness kept at bay.

She changed out of her sodden jeans into a loose pink dress and left her hair down and loose to dry. She found Adam Milroy some dry clothes and made up the bed in the spare room. Then she jointed a chicken and casseroled it with carrots, celery, bacon, onion, sherry and some tinned tomatoes and mushrooms. She set the kitchen table with one of her grandmother's damask cloths and laid out the old-fashioned bone-handled cutlery, two matching napkins in wooden holders, and finally the fragrant casserole and a dish of fluffy white rice and some fresh beans from the garden she'd picked that morning.

Before Adam had changed into her grandfather's clothes he had gone back down to fix up a feed bin in the garage for the mare and spread some more straw.

The clothes almost fitted him, because her grandfather had been as tall but broader around the midriff, so he had to wear an old leather belt about the waist, but the blue and white checked cotton shirt fitted well.

Surprisingly, although all through her preparations while he had been down with the horses and also checking the outside of the old house for damage she had worried about being shy and tongue-tied, they talked easily through the meal, mostly about horses, but pleasantly all the same.

And after it Adam paid her a compliment. 'That was delicious. I think you must know a lot about cookery already, Roz.'

'I—well, I enjoy it, and I've had plenty of practice.' She pushed her hair which had dried to a tangle of curls behind her ears and couldn't help beaming with pleasure. Then he insisted on helping her with the washing up and she made coffee and they took it into the lounge.

'You said,' he remarked as he lay sprawled back in a chintz-covered armchair, 'and I guess your prowess in the kitchen made me think of it, but you said this afternoon that you'd like to know how the economy worked, and computers. Were you serious?'

'Yes. Why?'

'Well, computers are something I happen to know rather a lot about,' he explained.

She looked surprised, and he explained about his business. She said, 'I've only ever associated you with horses. But if you think I could understand...'

He looked at her meditatively, then grinned suddenly and asked her for a pencil and paper.

An hour later Roz was rather amazed to find she did and was quite excited—so much so that she suddenly remembered the bottle of cumquat liqueur Mrs Howard had given them last Christmas, and suggested they try it to celebrate.

He laughed and looked speculative when she produced two small glasses of it and fresh coffee. He laughed some more when she took a sip that left her gasping and coughing.

'Oh! I had no idea it was so strong,' she spluttered at last, laughing too. 'Although I should have. Grandad used to say it would stun a horse, but I always thought he was teasing.'

She could never afterwards remember what pierced her feeling of warmth, enjoyment and security at that moment. It could have been wiping the cumquat liqueur-induced tears from her eyes and looking ruefully across at Adam Milroy wearing her grandfather's clothes, it could have been remembering him teasing Mrs Howard, but whatever it was, all of a sudden, like a swift passage from light to dark, all her burdens came back. Not only that, but she couldn't believe she could be laughing and joking when only a few miles away her beloved grandfather lay in a wet, desolate graveyard.

She put her glass down and stood up, turning away abruptly.

Adam Milroy watched her, young and slender and looking younger in the pink dress, with her shoulders shaking as she valiantly tried to control her emotions, and he sighed slightly, then stood up and went over to her.

'Roz ...'

'I'm sorry ... I'll be all right,' she gasped.

'You'd be better to cry it out. I don't mind.'

'No. No,' she whispered. 'I've done that. Now I've got to cope. He ... *he* wouldn't have wanted me to go to pieces, just to remember him with love.'

All the same, Adam put an arm around her again and she leant against him for a time, quietening.

Then he said that it had been a traumatic day and, tilting her face up to his and observing the shadows in her blue eyes, suggested she go to bed.

She agreed and thanked him. She asked him if there was anything else he would like, but he said no, he'd be fine and he'd take care of the lamps and check on the horses for the last time, so Roz found him a waterproof. Then she stood awkwardly for a moment before bidding him a grave goodnight.

Roz slept rather well, considering all her problems, and those that she'd not even thought of.

But when the Howards arrived home quite early the next morning, having heard the news of the hailstorm, they encountered not only the Electricity Board workers who had come to clear the tree and repair the line but Adam Milroy. It was obvious that it came as a slight shock to them all, but mostly Mr Howard, that Roz should have spent the night alone in the company of a strange man.

Mrs Howard recovered quickly, however—Adam had raised his eyebrows haughtily as the silence had lengthened once the explanations of his presence had sunk in—and she said that they had dashed home because they'd been worried about Roz, knowing she was on her own as well as worried about their own property, and she for one didn't believe Roz should *be* on her own yet, but it was so awkward with the foal, but Mr Milroy was not to be concerned, Roz would be coming back under their roof for the time being until . . . well . . .

whatever arrangements ... er ...

Mrs Howard ran out of breath then, which gave Adam the opportunity to commend that idea with a limited-version smile, and mention Roz's unfortunate encounter with Stan Hawkins the day before.

Mike immediately took Roz's hand and Mr Howard looked grimmer—he didn't hold with gambling of any sort, but Mrs Howard set her jaw and said, 'That does it. Pack a bag, Roz!' she commanded. 'And we'll move the mare and foal over too.'

Roz tried to protest, to no avail—and it was time to say goodbye to Adam Milroy again.

He seemed to hesitate, then observed, 'They say it never rains but it pours. I sincerely hope this is the end of it for you, young Roz, and that things improve from here on. Goodbye.'

'Goodbye. Thank you for everything.'

CHAPTER FOUR

Roz stirred restlessly and came back to the present with a sigh.

She could still hear sounds of revelry coming from downstairs and was surprised to see it was not yet midnight. She got up and glanced out of the window, to see that there were still three cars parked in the drive, Amy's, Angelo's and Richard's, and she was happy for Nicky that they had come to spend the evening with her, because she was pretty sure her sister-in-law had something rather weighty on her mind.

Just as I had, she thought, when I got coerced into going back to stay with the Howards after the hailstorm. Well, I hope Nicky's problems aren't as bad, and I don't see how they could be. If only I'd *known*!

She sighed again and sat down in the pink velvet covered armchair, plucking at the cording around the arm and letting her mind drift back again to the days after the hailstorm ...

The move had been accomplished without much fuss—Mrs Howard was like that, bright and bubbly but with a streak of competence and practicality that surprised one sometimes. She was also opposite in character to Mike's father, a dour man in whom the qualities of honesty and uprightness were clearly visible although a sense of fun was not. But he now owned his own fencing business and could afford to put Mike through college and live a moderately affluent life, although he had barely attended high school himself.

And despite his contempt for Roz's grandfather's passion for gambling, he had been a good neighbour over the years, one couldn't deny that. But the act of going back to stay with the Howards, to Mr Howard's visibly growing disapproval of his son's infatuation for Roz despite Mrs Howard's attempts to lighten the atmosphere, was a mistake, Roz knew, and she found herself regretting that night very much as she got ready for bed.

It had been an uncomfortable evening during which Mike had taken her for a walk after dinner, but when they got back it was as if Mr Howard knew that his son had taken her in his arms and kissed her fervently, and asked her to marry him.

Fortunately, she had made Mike see that it was something they couldn't rush into and made him promise not to mention it to his parents. But the truth of the matter was that she didn't know what to think herself, especially when out of the blue, as she was getting ready for bed, she found herself wondering whether the tragedy that had befallen her had tripped Mike's emotions into overdrive.

'Oh, God,' she whispered, 'what made me think that? He's been so wonderful and it's been ... well, I suppose we've been drifting towards this, but in other circumstances we wouldn't have ... we'd have been content to wait at least until he'd finished college, then got engaged perhaps and probably hoped his father got to like the idea better in the meantime.'

She rubbed her face wearily and sat down on the edge of the bed, wishing desperately that she was at home, spending an evening like she had the night before ...

She caught her breath and thought, how strange that

Adam Milroy should have come into her life twice, fleetingly, and that they should both be such memorable occasions. Because at fourteen, when most other girls had been worried about puppy fat but she had been gawky, he had driven into the stable yard to see her grandfather about a horse, and she had been struck virtually dumb.

She remembered it so clearly—the scarlet jumper she'd been wearing that Mrs Howard had knitted her, the patched jeans that were a bit too short for her, the long fair ponytails done up with red bobbles ... the bright cold day it was, the shiny foreign car, the tall, dark, handsome stranger wearing brown corduroy trousers and a tweed sports jacket over a black sweater who had climbed out of it. How he'd looked around and then his gaze had fallen on her with a bucket in one hand and a brush in the other, standing transfixed, and he had walked towards her and smiled that brilliant, crooked smile ...

At least, she amended to herself as she sat on the Howards' spare bed brushing her hair, *that* part she could remember so clearly, but the rest of his visit had passed in a sort of blur. She knew she'd hardly said a word, she knew she'd never felt more awkward or gawky as she'd led the horse around for his inspection, but that was all.

And what she had least expected was how from that time on, Adam Milroy would haunt her girlish daydreams and how she would for months build impossible fantasies around him.

Her grandfather hadn't helped, because after that visit he had enthusiastically sung Adam's praises and painted a word-portrait of him that had unknowingly fuelled Roz's dreams—he's worth a mint now, but when I first met him . . . all the same, he was impressive even then, you could see he was going to amount to something, *I* could anyway . . . knows horses inside out . . . I think he was married once but it didn't last, plenty of ladies in his life, though . . .

It was when her grandfather said that particularly that Roz unaccountably and childishly first thought of Adam Milroy as a Prince of Darkness. Strangely, though, it increased his attraction.

Of course not even the most ardent daydreams last for ever, and by the time she was sixteen she had begun to understand that women, especially very young ones, were very susceptible to the idea that they would be the one to reform some wildly attractive, sophisticated and experienced older man.

But although she had acknowledged this ruefully and discovered that her crushes were transferable, it had all worried her obscurely. Until the night Mike, of all people, had asked her to dance at the Grade Eleven party and instead of teasing her about something or other had said very seriously and embarrassedly that he liked her dress and thought she looked nice, *then* all of a sudden things had come right. She was like every girl she knew, with a boyfriend of her own and starting to fall in love.

And she was able to dismiss the curious problem of Adam Milroy with the wry thought that she had actually met her version of Harrison Ford or Michael Douglas.

'And now I've met him again,' she murmured aloud as she switched off the light and slipped into bed. 'Not that I'd be silly enough to even *wonder*, but life's strange. Not, for that matter, that I'm likely to meet him for a third time . . .'

* * *

But the next afternoon Mrs Howard received a phone call that made her strangely thoughtful for a time, then she asked Roz whether her appointment with the solicitor was for the next morning or the day after.

'The day after. Why?'

'Well, Roz, that was Adam Milroy on the phone. He's coming to see you tomorrow and he has some sort of a proposition for you—at least I assume so, because he asked me to ask you not to do anything about your grandfather's estate until he's seen you.'

'I don't understand,' Roz said bewilderdly.

'I'm not sure I do either,' Mrs Howard said slowly. 'But of course he does breed and race horses.'

Roz digested this and found it quite drove all other thoughts from her head. Including the nervous suggestion she had just been about to make to Mrs Howard that she should go home.

Much later that night she was to regret being deflected from that course, because Michael and his father had a row and it was impossible not to hear what was said in the heat of the moment.

'You're too young to even think of it, Mike! You haven't had a chance to . . . look around, to *grow up*. Do you think I relish the thought of having slaved for years to give you a good education just to see you throw it over the moon for some girl? . . . How can you expect to cope with college and a wife? I'm not going to support the two of you. Mike, she's not the one for you, she never will be, believe me, she's not the kind I would want for a son of mine . . .'

Someone knocked on Roz's door very early next morning, but guessing it was Mike she didn't respond because she just couldn't pretend she hadn't heard, and what could she say? So she waited until both Mike and his father had left the house and then went out, to find Mrs Howard sitting at the kitchen table looking unusually grim and pale.

'I . . . I'll go home today,' said Roz uncomfortably. 'I'm sorry and I . . . I don't know what to say. I'm *sorry*.'

Mrs Howard pursed her lips, then motioned her to sit down and poured her a cup of tea. 'Sorry is as sorry does, Roz, but I'm very angry, and I can't deny that. Not with you, though.'

'Who?' Roz whispered.

'*Men.*'

'Mike?'

'Mike's not a man.' Mrs Howard put the teapot down with a snap. 'He's a boy and he happens to be my only child, and I can't believe his father—I just can't believe him! To make such a fuss, such a dreadful issue of all this. I . . . I'm really so angry I don't know what to do!'

'Mrs Howard——' Roz began tremulously, but was interrupted.

'As if . . . as if it's not perfectly natural for a nineteen-year-old boy to think the love of his life has come upon him—why not try to ride it out? Why go through this hell . . .' She stopped and sighed. 'Sorry, Roz. I suppose you think the love of your life has come upon you, but . . .' She shrugged.

'Mrs Howard,' Roz began after a moment, then hesitated painfully.

'Go on.'

Roz twisted her hands. 'I can understand—well, that you think we're too young. But he said I'm not the right one for Mike and never will be. Is it because he's afraid

I'll be like my grandfather? Have some sort of a character flaw, like Grandad's gambling?'

Mrs Howard stared at her, then said wearily. 'My dear child, no. That's ridiculous, because we know you so well and you're so sane and sweet and a good girl, you really are. But . . .' She broke off.

'Please tell me,' Roz whispered.

Mrs Howard turned away and stared out of the window. 'It's . . . she turned back. 'It is something about you. Something that men find—well, let's say it wreaks havoc with their peace of mind. It's a sort of reserve and maturity together with your looks, your lovely body. It's . . . not going to be easy for you, Roz, nor perhaps for the man you marry. That's what Mike's dad is afraid of. You see, he's not—entirely unmoved by it himself.'

Roz's lips parted.

Mrs Howard watched her carefully. 'Do you understand what I'm trying to tell you, Roz?' she said after a moment.

'No . . . oh!' Roz's eyes widened with shock and she went pale.

'I see that you do,' Mrs Howard said quietly.

'But I had no idea! I—oh, please believe me, I . . .'

'Roz, Roz,' Mrs Howard said gently, 'don't upset yourself. Of course you had no idea. I don't want you thinking Mr Howard is something of a monster either. It only proves that he's a very human, middle-aged man—and sometimes it's a relief to know he *is* human,' she added with a grimace.

'But . . .'

'Unfortunately,' Mrs Howard continued, 'it's been very difficult for him to cope with this, as you can imagine, perhaps. He has a very strong moral streak and likes to take pride in his integrity. What,' she paused thoughtfully, 'never ceases to amaze me is how often people like that fall into a terrible trap. On top of which,' she said drily, 'men don't need much encouragement to shift the blame when it comes to women anyway, I've found.'

Roz stared at her. 'I don't understand,' she whispered.

'He blames you, Roz.'

'You mean ...' Roz's mouth fell open and her eyes were wide with disbelief and then appalled. 'But I've never ...'

'*I* know that, Roz.'

'I feel terrible. I feel ... do you really mean he thinks I ... encourage men to ... to ...' Roz stopped and licked her lips. 'Has he told you this?'

'Not in so many words, but I can read him like a book,' Mrs Howard said sadly. 'Nor did the fact that Adam Milroy spent the night, or what that other man threatened you with, help.'

'He didn't spend the night *with* me!' cried Roz.

'Sorry,' Mrs Howard closed her eyes briefly. 'Roz, how can I explain it better? It's ... like a defence mechanism Mr Howard is using against you—you can understand that? Oh, Roz, I'm sorry I ever had to tell you this, but circumstances have conspired against us and,' she sighed and looked considerably older suddenly, 'while I can't help but feel indignant about the way men treat us sometimes I ... at the moment I'm facing the prospect of a very real rift developing in this family.' She stared at Roz helplessly.

'What can we do?' Roz whispered after an age. 'I—I don't seem to be able to think too clearly. I mean, of course I'll go home, but Mike ... and ...' She blinked away some tears, her face white and distraught.

Mrs Howard stared at the tea pot, then visibly gathered herself. 'I'll think of something,' she said but with only a shadow of her normal decisive air. 'Why don't you have some breakfast and then change into something smarter—don't forget Adam Milroy is coming to see you this morning. I must say I'm very curious about that, aren't you?'

Roz stared.

'Had you forgotten?' Mrs Howard asked gently.

'I ... yes. But I don't feel hungry,' Roz said distractedly.

Mrs Howard took a dim view of that, however, and chivvied her into having toast and tea at least, then sent her off to get changed, but appeared moments later to help her choose her clothes. They settled, at least Mrs Howard settled, on a blue blouse that matched Roz's eyes and a full white cotton skirt. Then she suggested that Roz put her hair up and helped her to do it, remarking that it made her look very chic.

Later, over the next days and months, Roz was to wonder if Mrs Howard had had any inkling of what was on Adam's mind or any idea of what her revelations would do to Roz's state of mind, and seen a solution to their problems. But on the whole she rejected this thought. The years over which Mike's mother had treated her almost as a daughter made it difficult to believe... No, it had all been a coincidence, she decided each time.

But as she stared at herself in the mirror that morning it was the furthest thought from her mind. Because what she saw was a stranger, a girl she didn't seem to recognise, quite tall and slim about the waist, a girl *men* saw as a seductress and worse. A girl with a cloud of guilt and shame upon her mind and blue eyes that seemed to have gone beyond shock—something she was shortly to disprove.

'Why don't you take Mr Milroy down to see the foal, Roz?'

'He's seen her—'

'It would be no penance to see her again,' Adam Milroy said with a smile. 'It's also a lovely day.' He was casually dressed in khaki twill trousers, rather dusty leather boots and a plain white shirt open at the throat.

But Roz was having trouble concentrating on anything but trivia—such as why Mrs Howard should suggest she should change out of her jeans, only then to suggest she go for a hike across a paddock to find Nimmitabel and the old mare.

And not long out of the house her overburdened mind grasped some more trivia. It *was* a nice day, with the sky blue and clear and the hailstorm only a memory now. There was a gentle breeze stirring the peppercorns around the shed—and she rather wished she was dead.

She stopped walking abruptly out of sight of the house and said jerkily. 'I'm sorry, but I don't want to go any further. C-could you tell me what you wanted to see me about now?'

Adam stopped beside her and looked down at her with a frown between his eyes. 'What's happened? Has Stan Hawkins . . .'

'No! I haven't seen him again.'

'Then something's gone wrong here.'

Roz looked up at him in agitation. 'Please, if you could just . . .' But she couldn't go on.

They'd come to a fence, one of Mr Howard's neat, white painted fences, and Adam leant one elbow on the top rail and propped a dusty boot on the bottom one. Then he looked at her directly and said, 'All right, I've come to suggest that you and I get married, Roz.'

For a heart-stopping moment Roz thought the world had stopped and sent her spinning into space. What actually happened was that she stepped backwards in her utter amazement, tripped on a stone and all but fell before he caught her in his arms.

Then she realised he was laughing and she tried to twist herself free but couldn't, so she glared up at him and spluttered, 'If you think it's funny to make jokes about something like that, I don't!'

'Oh, I wasn't joking,' he drawled, but with his dark eyes still glinting with amusement. 'Nor was I laughing at you so much as myself. Well,' he added with a shrug, 'something like that.'

She stared up at him and could feel her heart beating wildly with shock; she didn't seem capable of leaving the protection of his arms. 'But it doesn't make sense! Why would you want to marry m-me?' she stammered. 'Especially if you find it so amusing, whatever the reason.'

'Roz,' he searched her troubled, totally bewildered face, drew her closer briefly, then let her go but took her hand and looked around, 'there's a bench over there. Come and sit down and discuss this with me.'

The bench was beneath an old willow tree and in some places the green leafy fronds nearly touched the ground, so it was a cool private spot. He kept hold of her hand as they sat down on the bench and stretched his free arm along the back of it.

'First of all,' he said presently, 'what I found amusing was that since I've made a lot of money I've had rather a lot of women . . . indicate to me that they'd be very happy for me to pop the question. Whereas you nearly fell down with shock. I found it refreshing and, I guess, ironic.'

'It shouldn't be ironic,' Roz said quietly. 'We barely know each other. It would be ironic if among all those women who've wanted to marry you, you found someone you desperately wanted but couldn't have.'

He smiled faintly. 'Point taken, my wise young friend.'

'I wasn't trying to be nasty or clever,' she said quickly.

Adam threaded his fingers through hers in silence. Then he said, 'I know. Another plus in your favour, Roz, but the fact remains I did find it so, even if all for the wrong reasons.'

She stirred restlessly, but her hand stayed in his. She said urgently. 'That's still no reason to want to marry me. Should . . . shouldn't people fall in love to want to marry?' She waited, then said anxiously, 'Don't you believe in love?'

'I believe,' he said meditatively, 'that a lot of people get married because they think they've fallen in love and then find it's not so. I believe it's very hard to differentiate between a physical attraction and that elusive thing they call love. I know that marriage is a dicey proposition at the best of times and that a cool, sane, level-headed approach could have a lot to recommend it.'

Roz shivered. 'I think that means you don't believe in love,' she whispered. 'And perhaps being so very rich hasn't helped, but I don't think it's a—well, a very good way to be.'

He released her hand and sat forward. 'Roz,' he said

levelly, 'when I was twenty I fell madly in love with a beautiful girl called Louise. We got married. Twelve months later we got divorced and she remarried an older, very rich man. It was possibly the best thing that could have happened. We ... thought we loved each other passionately, but in fact we just couldn't live together. I,' he paused, 'wasn't in the position then to give her much; she wasn't the kind of girl you could bury in a welter of overwork and all sorts of petty economies. She ...' He stopped and stared through the willow fronds. 'Yes, I am cynical about love,' he said eventually. 'It wouldn't be fair to tell you any otherwise. Not, though, because I still fancy I'm in love with Louise. But because *of* it and what's happened since. I think it might be a will-o'-the-wisp that people pursue endlessly and don't understand is only a fickle sort of thing, whereas an honest commitment of a practical nature ... serves one better.'

Roz opened her mouth, then shut it.

'For example,' Adam went on, 'and I apologise for being rather brutally honest on both counts—what I've said and what I'm about to say—Michael Howard is not for you, Roz. He's a kid, a nice kid probably, and I can't quarrel with his taste, but he's ...' he shrugged, 'like I was. Dazzled.'

'No,' she breathed, 'don't say that!'

He turned to her with suddenly narrowed eyes. 'Has he had any other girlfriends?'

'No—well, no, but ...' She managed to get her hand free.

'So you're the first for him and he's the first for you?'

'I ... *yes*, but ... you sound just like his father,' Roz said bitterly.

He took her hand again. 'If I were his father I'd be very

concerned,' he said, and added, 'also. Even though it was such a brief meeting yesterday, Roz, I could see the tensions barely beneath the surface.'

She turned her face to his. 'What tensions?'

'A father contemplating his son rushing into a marriage with his childhood sweetheart because circumstances have made her so vulnerable. A St George and the Dragon kind of situation, which is notoriously appealing to young men who are often more romantic at heart than they get credit for.'

Roz blinked and stilled at the echo his words evoked in her mind because, after all, hadn't she wondered the same thing?

'Was that all you saw?' she queried huskily after a moment.

Adam shrugged. 'His mother was valiantly trying to make the best of it, but I think that even fond as she is of you, she has her doubts too.'

'Everyone,' Roz said slowly, 'is more concerned that Mike's too young. I mean, you can't believe I'm too young to be married or you wouldn't be asking me, would you?'

He was silent.

'And the other thing is, we barely know each other!'

He smiled. 'Sometimes it's how you've got to know someone, not how long you've known them, that counts. I feel I know you rather well, as a matter of fact. I thought the same might have happened for you, but perhaps the last thing on earth you could imagine is us ... being married?'

Roz closed her eyes and tried to banish all her girlish fancies which chose to rise up and taunt her then most treacherously. And she had to think that if it wasn't all so impossible it was like a dream coming true—*would* have been, she amended, years ago. And she couldn't help the shaky laugh that rose to her lips, although she bit it off.

'What does that mean?' Adam asked. 'Yes or no? If you find me in the same league as Dracula, I'll go away now.'

'No, no, it's not that,' she said agitatedly. 'I . . . I don't know what to say. I'm . . .' She got up and away a few paces, then turned to him. '*Thank* you, because I think you mean well, but I couldn't. It wouldn't be right.'

'Roz,' he said abruptly, 'let me tell you what could be achieved if we got married. You'd have no problems with your grandfather's debts. You'd be able to keep Nimmitabel . . .'

'No!' she broke in incredulously. 'Is *that* what all this is about?'

'You could say, in part,' he replied drily, but there was a mocking look in his dark eyes as he added, 'But I can always get her when she comes up for sale. Being very rich does have its advantages.'

He waited and watched, and Roz wondered why she should feel guilty about what she'd said.

Adam went on when she could only stare at him confusedly, 'There'd be other advantages for you: you'd have security and a home—you mentioned that you'd like to have lots of children, and so, I find now, would I. Some, anyway!' He grinned, then sobered. 'And you'd also have a husband with your best interests at heart, and that I give you my word on, Roz. I may be an elderly cynic, but my word has always been my bond.'

'I . . .' she began helplessly.

'So far as the horse goes,' he said, 'I can't deny my interest in her, but what I'd like best is for *you* to be able to keep her. Perhaps,' he shrugged. 'I'm superstitious, but the two of you seem to go together—and before I live to regret saying that, if I didn't find you ... desirable I wouldn't be asking you to marry me if you came with six Nimmitabels.'

Roz blushed vividly.

'Perhaps you don't realise how lovely you are, Roz,' Adam told her quietly. 'Or how much *I'd* be gaining. A wife, admittedly young but with, I think, the intelligence and wisdom and grace to allow it to work. Someone I respect enough to want to have as the mother of my children—and before you ask me how I can know that I think it's probably because I've met you and known you when the chips are really down for you. That's generally a good test of character, and you, my dear, have come through with flying colours in my estimation.'

Roz opened her mouth, then closed it again. For the life of her she couldn't stop herself from thinking of the alternatives, of the damage she had so unwittingly wrought among the Howards, of Mrs Howard's pale, grim face and how she had been so kind over the years. Of Mike and how, until now, he had always got along so well with his father, of the curious fact that while she knew she was quite innocent she couldn't help feeling tainted by Mrs Howard's revelations.

'I . . .' She stopped and bit her lip, glancing at Adam to see that he watching her almost idly. As if he'd stated his case and was prepared for the outcome to go either way. And she thought suddenly how clean-cut and safe it sounded, with none of the dark secrets and pitfalls that apparently existed between men and women, as she had discovered this morning and found so shameful and frightening . . .

She thought of having to part with the foal, her home, she thought of Mike again and finally of Adam Milroy himself who had told her he respected her—also desired her, yes, she mused, but not in a way that made her feel degraded.

'I . . .' She looked up at last and he was still watching her carefully. 'All right. Yes. Thank you very much.'

Adam said nothing, just held out his hand to her, and she hesitated, then went back to the bench and sat down beside him. He put his arm around her shoulders because she'd started to shake and was horrified to find tears rolling down her cheeks that she couldn't control.

But he didn't seem to mind, in fact he pulled her head down gently on to his shoulder and stroked her hair as she cried with reaction to so much, a disastrous, horrifying couple of weeks in her life, a momentous step in her life.

Things moved then with a speed that took Roz's breath away.

She hadn't even seen Mike to explain, and felt cowardly but almost certain she would be unable to anyway. And Adam had broken the news to Mrs Howard there and then.

To her credit Mrs Howard had looked stunned and had started to say, 'Roz, if anything I said this morning . . .'

But Roz had gone up to her and put her arms around her as Adam had frowned and looked from one to the other of them probingly, and she'd said very quietly, 'I trust Adam—if I didn't I wouldn't be doing this, and I don't think I *am* the right one for Mike, otherwise I wouldn't be doing this either. Perhaps you could . . . help him to understand for me, *please*, and thank you for everything.'

'Oh, Roz!' Mrs Howard had appeared to do battle with herself, but finally she said, 'If you're very sure?'

'Very.'

But after a tearful parting and as they had driven to her grandfather's house, Adam had said, 'What did she say to you this morning, Roz?'

'Just . . . some of the things you said to me, about Mike, I mean.'

'I wondered if she might try to stop me rushing you away like this,' he'd said then with a faint smile.

So did I, thought Roz, but can I blame her for not? No. She was honest with me where many women might not have been, she was kind right up to the end when she could have turned on me . . . how could I ever blame her for putting her family first and understanding that this seems to be the only solution?

They had only called in at her own home briefly for Roz to mark the things she would like to keep, and it was from there that Adam arranged transport for the mare and foal.

'Oh, look, I only borrowed the mare,' she had said distractedly.

'Just give me the details and I'll buy her,' he had said calmly.

Then he had taken her to his flat in Brisbane which he used, he had told her, when he had to stay in town overnight. But he hadn't stayed with her. Instead, by nightfall, a cheerful person by the name of Milly Barker had arrived, and if she had thought it at all strange that she should have been summoned to play chaperon to

Adam Milroy's bride-to-be who was also a total stranger, all she'd said was, 'Oh, I'm so thrilled to meet you and I'm so excited! I'm Adam's housekeeper, by the way.'

'And she rules me with a rod of iron, incidentally,' Adam had put in with a grin.

'Oh ho! Well, you'll find out the truth about that soon enough, Roz—may I call you Roz?'

'Of course,' Roz had said shyly.

But over the next couple of days she had grown less shy with Milly Barker; it had been impossible not to as they'd shopped for a trousseau and Roz had discovered that Milly had no desire to probe beyond the face value of this marriage—or if she did, she suppressed it very well. Some months later she was to realise that Milly was much more than a housekeeper, that she ran Adam's social life and that, above all, she juggled his family with supreme tact and discretion. Although, Roz was also to think some time later, it must have tested even Milly to have had to bear the brunt of the family's shocked amazement when she had broken the news of the marriage. By which time Roz and Adam were married and on their way to North Queensland for their honeymoon.

What Adam had said to her on the subject of his family had been that he had no intention of allowing them any say in the matter, he never did anyway, nor of turning the occasion into some kind of a circus with everyone squabbling over who should be bridesmaids, groomsmen and heaven knew what.

'But your mother?' Roz had queried slowly. Milly had filled her in on the basics.

'My mother's got enough children to keep her in weddings for years to come—I'm only the second to do it so far—then we've got cousins and nieces and nephews ad infinitum, I sometimes think. But I've written her a letter for Milly to deliver. And among other things, I reminded her that my father persuaded her to run away from home to marry him and then presented her to the family as a *fait accompli*.'

'Oh.'

'Roz——' it had been the day before their simple register office wedding and they were having dinner that Milly had cooked them '—if you've discovered that you have any grave reservations about this, now is the time to tell me. I know you must have *some* reservations, but at least you know me a bit better now and should be able to make a more reasoned judgement.'

She had looked at him across the elegantly set candlelit table. 'Have you had some doubts?'

'No,' he'd said quietly but quite definitely.

Roz had lowered her lashes and remembered what she'd done the day before—checked in the Brisbane and the Gold Coast phone books and discovered that A. Milroy was listed in both and in the Brisbane one at the address of the flat. She had also known why she'd done it—if Mike had really wanted to find her it wouldn't have been difficult. But he hadn't, although ten days had elapsed. Perhaps it was foolish to expect him to understand, to wonder if he mightn't care for her more than all the obstacles in the world and find it impossible to let her do this. But he hadn't.

'No,' she'd said, 'neither have I.' And she'd smiled across the candle flame and asked him how Nimmitabel was settling down in her new home.

The same time the next evening they were on their honeymoon.

* * *

'Roz?'

'Mmm?'

'All right?'

'Yes. Fine,' she had said sleepily, and stirred in his arms and woke up a bit. 'Was it all right—I mean, was I any good?'

Their luxury hotel room in Cairns, their stepping-off point for a honeymoon exploring Far North Queensland, was silent.

Then Adam had said, 'You were all I expected you to be. Very sweet, a little scared, and even lovelier than I thought.' He ran his fingers slowly down her body.

'I thought it might hurt a lot more,' she had confided. 'I didn't really know what to expect.'

'I don't believe in hurting little young, scared creatures.'

'You make me sound like a rabbit,' she'd said indignantly but with a giggle. 'I'm not so little, am I?'

'Compared to me you are,' he had said gravely.

'But I mean—oh, you know what I mean ...' She broke off as his hand moved up to touch her breasts. 'Well, they're not very big, I know,' she had whispered, and felt her cheeks grow warm.

She had felt him laugh silently and had tensed, but he had held her closer and said, 'They're perfect, just like the rest of you—exquisite is the right word, I think, Roz.'

She had fallen asleep soon afterwards in his arms again, feeling almost lightheaded with relief, because it had taken all her nerve to go to bed with Adam Milroy and she had been sure she would be stiff with tension and—yes, doubt and disbelief. But as sleep had claimed her she was only able to be glad she had stuck to her decision to accept this side of married life and clamped down so hard on all her fears and uncertainties and tried to behave as a wife should straight away. Because in doing so she had discovered that she could handle it, that there was nothing specially terrifying about it and that Adam was patient and gentle and . . . just so nice.

And her last thought had been, anyway, if you marry someone for whatever reason it's only sensible to do your best, isn't it?

CHAPTER FIVE

'So what went wrong, Roz?'

Roz got up and crossed to the window. She sighed as the question she had asked herself seemed to echo around her beautiful bedroom at Little Werrington, and stared down at the moonlit driveway as Angelo appeared from beneath the veranda and jumped into his sporty little Datsun. Amy followed suit, but for a time it sounded as if her elderly car wasn't going to start, then it did reverberatingly, proclaiming to the world that it had a hole in the silencer.

Roz couldn't help smiling, because Amy was hopeless with cars, to the despair of her family, who were fond of saying she only had to look at one for it to go wrong. But Adam was very fond of Amy, she knew, and always said she had other, redeeming qualities, like her talent for music. But then Adam was very good with his young relatives—young things altogether, she thought, and if only I could have a baby ...

She pulled herself up and thought, no, be honest with yourself, Roz, that's a problem, but not the only one. So many things went wrong. Seeing that house on fire after our honeymoon on the way home from the airport ...

She bit her lip, remembering the sirens of the ambulances and the fire engines and another fire that had haunted her dreams from the day she had seen the second one until she wondered often if she would ever forget. And how those awful memories had kept the others alive, the Howards, Mr Howard ... that's what went wrong, she thought with sudden clarity as she waited for Richard to come out. I've been haunted by the spectre of falling in love with Adam—who doesn't believe in love anyway—haunted by the prospect of falling prey to those complex emotions that being really, physically attracted to someone seems to plunge you into ... I've been terrified by the way I've found myself wanting him, because after Mr Howard I hated the thought of it. But it's not only that, it's so much more—it must be, or why would I be feeling so unhappy and jealous and helpless? Why?

She rubbed her eyes wearily and whispered aloud starkly, 'You did fall in love with him, Roz, why won't you admit it? You not only want him but you need him, you're lost without him, and everything else you've ever tried to tell yourself means nothing. You thought *you* could direct your life with him, you thought you could keep a part of yourself aloof and untouched—you've *fought* him for the right to be able to do that, and only now, when you've achieved it, do you realise what a hollow victory it is. And you were so wrapped up in your memories and your problems you never stopped to think of him until it was too late. You even gave him cause to think you were still pining for Mike ... what a fool you were, Roz! Perhaps you even had a chance to ... make him feel the same way about you—and you just let it slip through your fingers ...'

She closed her eyes in pain.

When she opened them minutes later it was to focus on a curious little scene being played out down below beside Richard's car. She'd been so wrapped up in her own suffering she hadn't heard Richard come out of the house, but he undoubtedly had, also Nicky, and they were now embracing passionately in the moonlight and there was nothing cousinly about it at all.

Then Richard put Nicky away from him, but even from a distance Roz could see the effort it cost him, just as she could see tears glinting on Nicky's face.

'Oh!' she framed the word silently as everything fell into place. Margaret had seen this coming—so had Flavia! It had been Richard and Nicky she'd meant on the night of Roz's birthday party, not Angelo and his new girlfriend. And the things Nicky herself had said—if only she knew where Adam stood, for example.

Roz blinked rapidly, then moved away from the window because she felt as if she was trespassing, but anyway she heard the car start up and drive away within moments.

But the question remained—where would Adam stand?

Would he share Margaret's viewpoint that Richard was not what Nicky should have? Or Flavia's theory that they were only babies—everyone's concern no doubt because they were cousins? But they're not really, she thought, they're only second cousins. Margaret and Nicky are cousins. That's not so bad, surely?

But with a feeling of chill in her heart, she decided that Adam was not going to like the idea of Richard and his sister Nicky, and the thought of it was another burden she took to bed with her.

'Roz, you look pale,' her mother-in-law said to her the next morning. Roz had forgotten Flavia was coming until Milly had reminded her at breakfast, which Nicky had not come down for.

'I think I'm missing Adam,' Roz replied, and winced inwardly as Flavia immediately looked gratified. Then she asked where Nicky was.

'Still asleep,' said Roz ruefully.

'But it's eleven o'clock!'

'She had a late night last night and she is on holiday, so I thought I'd let her sleep in. I'm afraid I slept in as well.'

'She went out?'

'No. Angelo came down, and Amy and . . .'

'Ah, that's good,' Flavia pronounced. 'I like to see them all together, and you know, it amazes me what good friends Angelo and Nicola are now, considering that they fought like little tigers all the time they were growing up. Not that I can believe she's nearly grown up, but the I'm probably a silly old fool. And thank you for having her to stay, Roz,' she said warmly, and patted Roz's cheek. Then she drifted over to the window and added, 'Goodness me, you have more visitors, Roz! Margaret, by the look of it and—why, yes, I do believe she has Elspeth with her!'

Roz stared and closed her eyes briefly in horror, for it was indeed Margaret, and as she often did, she had brought Aunt Elspeth with her. But I'm sure I told her Flavia was coming today, Roz thought distractedly. Because it was a well known fact that Flavia and Elspeth detested each other and at times, less than cordially.

'Um,' she said,' I did mention to Margaret that you were coming today. She must have got the dates mixed up . . .'

'Not at all!' Flavia said sweetly. 'There's no reason for Margaret and Elspeth to stay away because I am here. I shall even go out and greet them!'

'I'll ... I'll just have a word with Milly about lunch,' said Roz, and fled.

'Oh, Milly,' she panted breathlessly, bumping into her in the kitchen, 'help!'

'What is it?'

Roz told her, and even Milly looked comically concerned for a moment. The she said, 'You can cope. Just be regal, and mention Adam frequently—that always does the trick, I've found. What about Nicky? Want me to wake her up?'

'Yes, her mother will be wondering—but I'll do it. Would you mind holding the fort while I dash upstairs?'

There was nothing comical about Nicky's reaction as Roz gently shook her awake and broke the news to her. 'Oh no!' she groaned, and pulled the pillow over her head. 'Oh, God, what have I done to deserve this?' She thrust the pillow aside and sat up. 'If they've all come to ...'

'They haven't,' said Roz, and immediately realised she'd made a slip, but Nicky seemed not to notice, so she went on, 'I mean, Margaret must have mixed the dates up, because I'm sure she wouldn't have brought ...'

'Roz, the last thing I feel like dealing with today is Mummy and Aunt Elspeth, *sparring* at each other, and as for Aunt Margaret——! Can't you ...?'

'No, Nicky,' Roz said gently. 'It's too late for that. Just be cool, calm and collected and mention Adam *frequently*. That always does the trick.'

Nicky looked at her with a suddenly speculative gleam in her, and Roz held her breath, but her sister-in-law said with a grin, 'I've heard that somewhere before. Oh well, I suppose it could be worse. Lucia could have come too!'

* * *

'Oh, Roz,' said Nicky hours later when the protagonists had departed, 'you *must* admit we're a mad family. I nearly died when Mum and Aunt Elspeth got into that conversation about the merits of Anglo-Saxon qualities of character over Latin ones. I mean, I nearly died trying not to laugh. They were so polite and so lethal—and they've been fighting that particular war ever since they met, can you believe it?'

'I can now,' said Roz with a grin.

'But you were great, you really gave them something to think about when you said you thought they mixed marvellously well and wasn't Adam living proof of it. That stopped them in their tracks!'

'I suspect not for long,' Roz said wryly. 'As soon as I said it I could just picture Elspeth saying—yes, but it's his Anglo-Saxon genes that have tempered his Latin ones. Or your mother saying—ah, but he might have turned out to be a real cold cod without my genes!'

'Cold cod!' Nicky started to laugh again.

'Sorry, I wasn't trying to make fun of your mother,' Roz said ruefully. 'I like and admire her.'

'Do you, Roz?' said Nicky slowly.

Roz hesitated, then said honestly. 'I was always rather nervous about how she—well, viewed me. Now I know she ... doesn't disapprove of me I suppose it's easy to say I think she's very human and warm and funny and caring, but I do ... I've thought that for some time. Why do you ask, Nicky?'

'No reason. It's just that if she were younger she might ...'

'Fifty-five isn't terribly old, Nicky.'

'No, but if I was her first child she might only be thirty-eight ...' Nicky stopped and looked conscience-stricken and anxious. 'It's not that I don't love her and admire her and respect her, Roz, but some of her ideas are terribly old-fashioned.'

'I think,' Roz said carefully, 'most mothers are like that, or seem to be. By the time we're mothers,' she bit her lip, 'we'll probably be the same. I suppose they do know all the pitfalls.'

'They can certainly think of plenty—behind every tree, they are, if mothers are to be believed,' Nicky said darkly.

Roz waited with a feeling of inevitability, but Nicky only remarked, 'Aunt Margaret was quiet today.'

'Yes.'

'Well, what's on tomorrow? When's Adam due back, by the way?'

'The day after tomorrow. And Les is taking Nimmitabel to the races tomorrow, just to accustom her to all the noise and excitement. How would it be if we got out our glad rags and went along?'

'I didn't really bring anything in the glad-rag line,' Nicky said ruefully.

'Then let's go and inspect my wardrobe this minute!' said Roz. 'We're not much different in size.'

She couldn't help feeling relieved when Nicky jumped up enthusiastically, all her problems seemingly forgotten. But she did wonder if it wasn't cowardly to be hoping against hope that Nicky wouldn't confide in her.

Her hopes were dashed the next evening.

Nicky appeared to enjoy her day at the races and she looked stunning in a rose pink tunic outfit of Roz's. Roz herself wore pale ice blue, and at one stage Nicky even said to her, with her dark eyes sparkling wickedly, 'You and I are creating a lot of interest, Mrs Milroy! *Male* interest. Isn't it lucky we contrast so well?'

Roz agreed, and immediately thought that perhaps Nicky's problems weren't so serious after all.

But when they got home, Nicky seemed not to be able to sit still after dinner, and she finally dragged Roz out for a set of tennis under the floodlights. 'We can have a swim afterwards,' she said energetically, and added teasingly, 'What's the point of having all these floodlit facilities if you don't use them?'

'Adam and Roz use them frequently,' said Milly.

'Good,' Nicky said briskly, although she knew this as well as Milly. And Roz and Milly exchanged rueful glances.

They didn't complete a game, however, before Nicky threw her racquet away and sat down suddenly on the court with her head in her hands. Roz came round the net, picked up Nicky's racquet, found herself wondering if Milly was still home to help her with this crisis, but Milly had gone to visit friends in Nerang ...

'Nicky,' she said quietly, 'come inside. We can talk more comfortably there.'

Nicky's shoulders shook and for a time she ignored Roz, then she stumbled up, and Roz took her hand.

In the den, Roz dimmed the lights and said, 'Now tell me. It's Richard, isn't it?'

'Yes,' Nicky wept. 'But how did you know?'

'I saw you the night before last. I wasn't spying on you, but I couldn't sleep and I was standing at the window, that's all.'

'And you never said a word!' Nicky marvelled bitterly, looking up and displaying a tear-streaked, dirty, woebegone face.

'I thought ... if you wanted to tell me you would. Nicky, does everyone else know?'

'Of course they know,' Nicky said even more bitterly. 'If you know a way of keeping a secret from this damn family of ours, I wish you'd tell me what it is!'

'But—does that mean you haven't confided in anyone?'

'I haven't had to. And nobody's come out and admitted they know, but I keep getting these well-meaning remarks from everyone on the dangers of marrying young, the dangers of marrying cousins—although he's not really a cousin—how I should get my degree first and sample life a bit more—that really riled me, Roz, because if I did go out and sample life they'd be the first to be filled with horror, I bet you! I even had a lecture from Mum about how notoriously unreliable one's first love generally turned out to be. And yet when I was little she used to boast about Dad being the first and only love of her live, and she got married when she was *eighteen*!'

Roz grimaced inwardly. 'Is Richard your first love, Nicky?'

'Yes. Oh, I've had some boyfriends, but I never got serious with any of them. You know how it is, you go out with a boy and then when he tries anything, you just know it's not on. But with Richard it's different, it's as simple as that.'

'Nicky, you asked me the other day whether Adam was my first love and I told you . . .'

'I know,' Nicky interrupted. 'But one shouldn't generalise! I mean, there are no hard and fast rules, are there?'

'No,' Roz admitted, 'but I think there's probably a . . . a sort of dangerous age when you *feel* competent to make these decisions and only realise later that you weren't—Nicky . . .'

'Roz, although it wasn't the first time for you, you weren't any older than I am when you fell in love with Adam.'

'But Adam was a lot older than Richard,' Roz reminded her, yet she thought, oh *hell*, I'm trying to give advice from a horribly false position.

'Perhaps, but how long did it take you to make up your mind about Adam?' queried Nicky.

Five minutes—no, at least half an hour, Roz reflected, and was silent for a time. 'I suppose,' she said at last, 'what I'm trying to say is that in the end you have to make up your own mind but it's *not* wise to rush into it, Nicky, and I think that probably applies to any age.'

Nicky glanced at her miserably. 'Would you . . . could I ask you a favour, Roz? Would you sort of bring the subject up with Adam? I know it's a lot to ask, but at least if I knew he wasn't worried about us being second cousins—well, then I wouldn't care what the rest of them thought.'

'I'm sure you could talk to Adam about it yourself, Nicky.'

'I don't know why, but I just can't seem to pluck up the courage,' Nicky admitted. 'And I've thought he's been rather—I don't know—preoccupied lately, which is probably why he hasn't found out. He and Lucia are the only two who don't know now, but I think everyone's been working hard to keep it from *her*, because she'd have a fit. Nothing short of a title would satisfy her social climbing aspirations these days, although where on earth she expects me to find that, I can't imagine.'

Roz smiled mechanically because she was thinking

how odd it was that Nicky should have noticed that Adam was preoccupied when *she* hadn't. How wrapped up in myself I must have been, she thought.

'Also,' Nicky went on earnestly, 'you'd have the advantage of being able to point to yourself and say— well, I was only nineteen.'

Roz sighed inwardly. But a look at Nicky's unhappy but stubborn young face reminded her of Margaret's prediction. 'All right,' she said abruptly. 'Just don't do anything rash in the meantime.'

'There's not much chance of that,' Nicky said gloomily. 'Even Richard . . .' She stopped.

'What about Richard?'

'Well, he says he'd rather wait until we get everyone's approval. But that's impossible, because I've never known them all to agree on *anything*.'

'What about Angelo and Amy?' asked Roz. 'What do they think?'

'They can't see anything wrong with it. They *know* how well suited Richard and I are.'

The next morning Roz went down to ride Nimmitabel, but found that Les was giving her the day off.

'Anything wrong, Les?' she asked anxiously.

He rolled his eyes. 'No, Roz, she's just a shade off her tucker, but that's because we wormed her yesterday. I'm not taking any chances, though. Incidentally, she's decided to take exception to being wormed, she played up something shocking.'

Roz laughed. 'There are some horses who just object to having a tube stuck down their nostrils into their stomach, Les,' she said teasingly.

'I know it,' he conceded, 'but she never has before. I

got the feeling she was just being capricious, if not to say downright pigheaded. Still, now we know it, we'll either tranquillise her the next time or resort to paste. And in the meantime a day off isn't going to hurt her, she's coming along real well, Roz.'

Roz went back happily to the house and encountered Milly, who reminded her that she had an appointment with her obstetrician.

'Oh,' said Roz, disconcerted, 'I'd forgotten—I seem to be awfully forgetful at the moment, and anyway, there doesn't seem any point. Could you cancel it for me, Milly?'

Milly removed her glasses, a sure sign of disapproval. She was also the only person other than Adam who knew that Roz was seeing an obstetrician. 'What do you mean, there doesn't seem to be any point, Roz?'

'I . . . nothing,' Roz said hastily.

'He did tell you it was necessary for him to see you regularly for a time, didn't he, Roz? And Adam . . .'

'I'll go, I'll go,' Roz broke in wryly. 'Just don't tell Nicky why I'm going to the doctor or what kind of . . .'

'Who's going to the doctor?' asked Nicky, wandering into the kitchen. She looked a little pale, Roz thought, but calm.

'I am. Just for a check-up,' she said brightly. 'Want to come into town with me? You could do some window-shopping and we could have lunch.'

But Nicky decided to stay at home and improve her suntan round the pool. For a moment Roz was tempted to take Milly into her confidence in case anything came up while she was away, but mainly because she had to hurry to get ready and because she couldn't imagine what could come up, she didn't.

* * *

Mr Mason was grey-haired and fatherly, and he went out of his way to cause her the minimum of discomfort and distress.

Afterwards he said to her, 'Well, Roz, I think I can say now that there appears to be no physical problem. There's a slightly irregular pattern to your ovulation, but many women suffer that, and indeed, many women overestimate their fertility. Which brings us back to what might be affecting you—tension and anxiety. Are you still having the nightmares?'

'No . . . at least not for a while,' she answered, and it struck her ironically that she might have too much else to worry about at the moment.

'That's good. Now here's what I'm going to suggest. No more tests, no more visits—I want you to go home and forget about getting pregnant for at least six months.'

Roz smiled faintly and he looked at her enquiringly. 'Adam,' she hesitated, 'agrees with you.'

'Adam's been very good about it, Roz. A lot of men find it difficult to accept that they could be the cause of the problem, but he said to me that if you were prepared to go through this the least he could do was participate himself. You do realise you're more concerned about this than he is?'

'I . . . yes.'

'And I know I've explained to you before about tension and anxiety, which is why I want you to go home now and really try to take my advice.'

'I'll try—no, I will,' she promised.

'Because it's like a vicious circle, you see, Roz. I mean, the news is good—I know two years of trying to conceive probably seems like a lifetime to you, but you could well be prolonging it by worrying so much. You have to break the circle.'

Why couldn't I tell him that's already been done? Roz wondered as she steered her little blue sports car down the Pacific Highway. Only Adam broke it, but in doing so he seems to have started me on another one.

But while she had been able to confide in Mr Mason about her nightmares, she had not been able to about the true state of her marriage. How could you tell anyone that? Especially when you'd been deluding yourself about it and had not known the stark truth of why you wanted Adam Milroy's baby so much. Not to pay off a debt, not to keep your half of the bargain, but because you loved him.

She blinked away some tears and pondered again the awful irony that now she knew there was no physical impediment, and now she'd sorted out her inner torment, she couldn't put it to the test.

I could just tell Adam, she mused. I could tell him that the scales just seemed to fall from my eyes, that his proposition jolted me out of all the self-deceptions I was practising. Only I don't know if it's what he wants to hear, if it's not too late, if there isn't another woman...

So many ifs, and he's coming home tonight and I don't know what to do!

Unfortunately all this made Roz less sensitive to Nicky. Then, Adam didn't arrive when expected, and when Milly rang the airport it was to discover that his flight from Tokyo had been delayed in Manila.

That was when Milly decided to take charge. 'It could be well past midnight by the time he gets home and he might even decide to stay in Brisbane, so we'll go to bed. You're looking tired anyway, Roz.'

'I'm certainly feeling tired!' sighed Nicky with a large yawn. 'Must be this country air,' she added almost hastily, and it was only later, much later, that both Milly and Roz were to remember how warmly she had kissed them both goodnight.

'Oh,' said Milly as the door closed behind Nicky, then, 'no, it doesn't matter.'

'What?' Roz asked.

'Well, I popped over to Pimpama this morning, to the post office, and just as I was about to drive off I heard the phone ring, but Nicky took it. I forgot all about it, but it couldn't have been anything important. Jeanette gets back tomorrow.'

'Yes, and I suppose we'll get back into full swing.' Roz grimaced. 'I think I will go to bed, Milly. But what if Adam rings?'

'I'll switch the phone through to my bedroom. Goodnight, Roz. I was *so* pleased to hear your news!'

But half an hour later, Roz realised to her despair that she wasn't going to fall asleep.

Finally she wandered into Adam's bedroom. It was more austerely furnished than hers, with built-in drawers and cupboards but a more vivid colour scheme, emerald green wallpaper, a matching carpet with an inset rectangular band of a rich yellowy cream that matched the box-fitted bedspread.

She moved around for a time, touching his things, the silver-framed photo of his father beside the bed, the onyx-backed brush set Nicky and Angelo had saved for years, so they'd claimed, to buy him for a birthday, the carved wooden box he kept his cuff-links in.

She fiddled with the cuff-links for a time, then put them back in the box with a sigh and glance at herself in the square mirror above the built-in dressing table. She wore a pair of white, self-patterned silk pyjamas with short cap sleeves, and although they were almost tailored in design the silk was rich and lustrous and sensuous.

But Adam's presence was so strong in this room, she could feel her half-formulated impulse, that was definitely associated with her beautiful pyjamas, wavering.

She turned away and then, consumed by another impulse, folded back his bedcover and lay down on his bed—wondering what skills beautiful geishas possessed that she might not, and how she could acquire them and make herself so desirable to Adam he wouldn't be able to resist her. Because if he didn't want to hear what she had to tell him, she knew she would be no match for him with mere words.

So here I am, she reflected sadly, a wife of two years, wondering how to seduce her husband, how to take the initiative, which I've never done before—feeling like a girl before her first time . . .

She fell asleep with all these thoughts on her mind, only to wake up disorientated and drowsy, and with Adam leaning over her.

CHAPTER SIX

HER LIPS parted and she stared up into Adam's dark eyes and wondered for a moment if she was dreaming.

Then she sighed, a tiny little sound, and without conscious volition her arms slid up around his neck. 'You came back,' she whispered.

'Of course—did you doubt it, Roz?'

'Yes. No. I mean, you must be tired. I don't know if it's much fun to be stranded in Manila at the moment. Oh, you're changed already,' she said softly and confusedly as she realised he had his towelling bathrobe on.

'I've had a shower, and it was no fun being stranded in Manila, but mainly because it was one of those flights destined to go wrong—my luggage appears to have disappeared and I feel frustrated beyond words with airlines and their bloody silly baggage-handling systems—but I didn't mean to wake you. You seemed to be sleeping so peacefully I was going to sleep in your bed.'

Roz considered this and the harsh, tired lines of his face and the clean, tangy smell of him although his jaw was dark, and felt her heart contract. 'Now . . . now that I'm awake, won't you stay with me?' she whispered, and slid her hands beneath his robe.

'Roz . . .' he began tautly.

'I know, I know we have an agreement,' she said huskily, exploring the supple skin of his wide shoulders beneath his robe, 'but we could always start again tomorrow if you wanted to. I would ... it's just that I would ... love to be loved right now, and you might be able to relax and ...'

'*Loved?*' he echoed.

She stared up at him and her heart started to beat uncomfortably. She swallowed and thought with fright that she'd blundered unforgivably again and either desperation or the thoughts she'd entertained before she'd fallen asleep had betrayed her. Then as the silence lengthened, fear hardened into certainty and she withdrew her hands and sat up as he moved back. 'It doesn't matter. Are you hungry? Would you like a snack?'

'No. Roz ...'

But she interrupted him. 'It's all right—I understand.'

He said, 'What do you understand?'

'That it's,' she turned her head to look at his bedside clock, 'three in the morning, that you've been flying for hours and hours and then driving on top of it.' She shrugged. 'That's enough, isn't it? To make you feel like a zombie or something? But seriously, if you'd like something to eat ...'

'Milly left something out for me.'

'What would we ever do without Milly?' Roz said lightly. 'Well, I'll get back to my own bed. Sleep well!' She went to slide off the bed, but he caught her wrist.

'Considering that's the first offer I've ever had from you, Roz,' he said, his lips barely moving and his eyes as dark as the night outside the small pool of lamplight that encircled them, 'I'd be a fool to knock it back.'

She took a breath as that dark gaze travelled from her loose dishevelled hair to her lips, her eyes which were wide and disconcerted, then down the sleek white silk to her outlined breasts.

'But if you don't want it,' she whispered, 'what are you knocking back? Nothing of value . . .' She broke off and winced, realising she'd spoken reproachfully, as if she had any right to be that, and because she'd wanted composure and found instead only a tattered kind of dignity. She looked away awkwardly.

Adam was examining her meditatively when she looked back at last, still holding her wrist in his long fingers. Then he remarked, 'I'm afraid you've hit the nail on the head, Roz.'

'Oh!' she gasped, and her eyes were stunned and hurt.

He smiled grimly. 'We could make it worthwhile, though,' he drawled. 'You could tell me if you have an ulterior motive—is the gilded cage not so bad after all? Or is the prospect of being an *unkept* woman rather terrifying suddenly? Or did you just wake up feeling sexy and find me . . . on hand? They might none of those be the best reasons to want to make love, but at least they'd be honest.'

Roz stared at him as if mesmerised, and for a moment she hated him. Then she realised with dull despair that he was entitled to think any or all of those things. And to tell him now that she loved him could only sound false, because she'd left it too late, said too much, done to little . . .

'Adam, is there someone else?'

If it was any satisfaction to her, which it wasn't, she saw that she'd surprised him. His eyes narrowed and his fingers tightened cruelly around her wrist before he released it abruptly.

She rubbed it mechanically and waited with baited breath.

'What makes you think that, Roz?' he said finally with a spark of anger in his eyes that frightened her. 'And are you only asking that or *hoping* it?'

'No! I'm sorry, I shouldn't ... I ...' She stopped and made a helpless little gesture. 'I'll go to bed.'

'And hope that in the morning things will have sorted themselves out?' he mocked.

She trembled and said huskily, 'I think you expect an awful lot sometimes, Adam ...' Only to wonder immediately why she'd said it. Yet wasn't it true that he'd married her without loving her and everything came back to that? Yes.

She tilted her chin and started to say goodnight, but he interrupted her. 'Do I, Roz? Perhaps. Goodnight.'

Roz slipped into her own bed feeling exhausted and drained, her moment of defiance gone, and fell into an uneasy sleep until about eight o'clock when the sound of raised voices woke her. This was so unusual she sat up in alarm—and realised the voices were coming closer and she could hear Milly saying, 'She must have done it between the time I went to bed and you came home, or maybe later, I don't know, but I didn't hear a thing. Was her car in the garage when you ...?'

'I didn't park my car in the garage, I didn't even open the doors!' Adam said furiously then. 'I left it out front, where it still is if you'd care to look. Nor did I think to check her bed, but the real mystery to me is how this could have all blown up without you or Roz being ...'

The voices stopped outside her bedroom door, then it

opened violently and Adam stood in the doorway with a piece of paper in his hands and an expression of such anger on his face that Roz put her hand to her throat fearfully and stammered, 'What is it?' although she had an incredulous inkling.

He shut the door sharply behind him, but not before Roz saw Milly standing in the passage, her face white and worried.

'Read this,' said Adam through his teeth, and strode over to the bed to thrust the piece of paper at her. He was dressed in jeans and a T-shirt.

'What is it?'

'As if you don't know,' he said sardonically, and took the paper back. 'I'll read it—it's from Nicky, and it was on the hall table. "*Dear* Roz, I hope you don't think this is cowardly of me leaving you to explain things to Adam, but I've decided to take your advice. You did say I would have to make up my own mind. Well, I have. I want to marry Richard . . ."' he broke off, exclaimed violently, *'Richard!* I don't believe it!'

'Go on,' Roz said. 'Is there more?'

'Oh yes! She says ". . . and if the family don't approve they'll never see me again." She then,' he went on with such withering scorn that Roz blanched, 'goes through detailed instructions about how we're to place an advertisement in the personal column of a newspaper to signify our approval.'

'She . . . I . . .' Roz put her hands to her mouth, because if she'd thought he looked angry last night it was nothing to how he was looking at her now.

'You?' he queried, then when she couldn't speak, 'Don't worry, I just know I have you to thank for this,

Roz. Were you trying to relive your life through Nicky when you gave her your advice? Were you thinking longingly of Mike Howard, the great love of your life that you let slip through your fingers because everyone told you he was too young, but most particularly me?'

'No! No, you don't understand,' Roz cried.

'Then Nicky's lying? You never said that to her?' he grated.

'No! Yes, I did, but ...'

'Then you'll pay for this, Roz,' he said in the hardest voice she'd ever heard.

'Adam, you don't understand. It wasn't like that at all!'

'Oh, but I do,' he said with soft menace. 'And so will you shortly.' He walked out and slammed the door.

Roz scrambled out of bed to go after him, then she hesitated and decided to get dressed first. At random she pulled on a pair of jeans and a pink cotton blouse which she was still buttoning as she ran downstairs.

The kitchen was empty, so she tried Adam's study and he was there with Milly, talking into the phone, to Margaret she guessed as he said, 'I want Richard down here within an hour, and if you can lay your hands on Amy bring her too. No buts, Margaret, just come.' He slammed the phone down and glanced at Roz.

'Well?' he said in such a hard, clipped voice that Milly did an indiscreet double-take.

'Adam,' Roz said shakily, 'please, you must believe me, I warned her not to do anything rash. I only ever knew about it accidentally in the first place, although I could see she had something on her mind. But the night before last she broke down and told me. And so I ...'

'Gave her your famous advice?'

'*No!* I tried to give her the opposite advice, actually. But she kept pointing out that I'd only been nineteen and that I barely knew you. Then,' Roz took a breath, 'she asked me to speak to you about it. I said *she* should, but she said she couldn't pluck up the courage. That's when I said I would so long as she didn't do anything rash in the meantime. I *swear* that's how it was. Something must have happened yesterday . . .' She broke off abruptly and looked at Milly. 'That phone call . . .?'

'Yes,' Milly said slowly. 'Now I wonder . . .' She broke off to explain to Adam, then added, 'The more I think about it the surer I am that phone call sparked this off. She was quiet yesterday, Roz. And then she said she was so tired, but she did nothing all day really. While you were away she just . . .'

'And where the hell were you?' Adam shot at Roz.

She flushed at his tone. 'At the doctor's,' she said steadily.

'So who the devil do you think rang her and upset her?' he demanded.

Roz lifted her shoulders helplessly. 'I can only guess. Perhaps Lucia's found out now—Nicky did say you and Lucia were the only two who didn't know.'

'Do you mean to tell me the whole family has known about this and not bothered to enlighten me?' he demanded with quiet fury. 'And that you, knowing this was on the cards, made no move to alert anyone, Roz?'

'I'm trying to make you understand I didn't know she was going to do this. And I was going to tell *you*. I just didn't . . . have a chance.'

'But you had her here with you, you knew she was in a state—you must know by now how volatile Nicky is! My dear Roz, even if only subconsciously I think she must have gained some encouragement from you. Perhaps it even supplied you with that ulterior motive last night,' he said with irony. 'Were you worried that you might have set something in motion that could be a little hard to explain?' he finished between his teeth.

Roz stood as still as a statue, while Milly looked as if she wished she could disappear into a hole in the ground, but it was obvious Adam couldn't care less, because he said then, 'Well, just for the record, let's hear what you would do if you were in my shoes, Roz?'

Roz licked her lips and discovered she was angry. 'If I were you, Adam, I'd put the ad she wants in the paper right away. And when she comes back I'd let them get engaged. I don't *know* whether marriage would work out for them or if he's the right one for Nicky, but personally I think she could do a lot worse, and I don't really think it's a crime to marry your second cousin. But apart from that I think you could trust Richard to behave sensibly—he told her he wouldn't marry her without the family's approval, and I think you'll find he will be just as stunned as the rest of us are that she's done this. So if I were you, Adam, that's what I'd do. Tell them you don't object to them being engaged and if in,' she shrugged, 'a year they still feel the same way, then you will discuss marriage. I don't see how else you can handle Nicky, and anyway, not *all* young marriages fail, although I agree they'd be wise to wait.'

'I . . . actually I agree with Roz,' Milly said awkwardly.

Adam was silent and his dark eyes held Roz's blue gaze captive. But she didn't flinch, just returned his stare calmly, her lips set and something saying inside her head, make what you will of that, Adam Milroy!

He did. 'I don't suppose I could have expected anything else from you, Roz.'

Something snapped inside her. 'Nor I from you!' And she turned and ran from the room, just as the phone started to ring.

She ran upstairs to her bedroom and closed the door, then leant back against it panting with anger, frustration and battling a tidal wave of tears. I can't stand much more, she thought. I do ... I do hate him after all. And the time's come to do something about it!

She went over to her dressing room and heaving down a suitcase from the top shelf, dragged it over to the bed. Then she pulled open her bureau drawers and indiscriminately gathered a cloud of underwear into her arms.

The door opened and she glared across the room at Adam as he came in and closed it behind him. 'Go away,' she said huskily, and pushed her hair which she'd not had time to brush off her forehead, dropping drifts of delicate colour around her—ivory, cyclamen, pale grey.

'What do you think you're doing?'

'What does it look as if I'm doing? I'm packing and I'm leaving. I may not be the kind of wife you thought you could make me into, and while I take some of the responsibility for that, I don't have to be insulted in front of other people or accused of the things you've accused me of this morning. Everyone's allowed one mistake in their lives, Adam, and I'm obviously yours. Why don't you just admit it and let me go? You can keep Nimmitabel as payment for all you've done for me, but ...' She stopped and backed away a step as he came right up to her and wrested what she had left in her arms away.

'Adam,' she said hoarsely.

'You're going nowhere, Roz,' he said quietly.

'I am! You can't stop me . . .'

'Oh yes, I can.' He took her into his arms and she struggled desperately and with tears pouring down her cheeks, but with futility, until her strength ran out abruptly and she could only lean against him helplessly, shaking and crying. He lifted a hand and pushed her hair away from her hot, wet cheek, then picked her up and carried her over to the bed.

'N-no . . .' she stammered.

'What did the doctor have to say yesterday?' he asked, surprising her into immobility as he put her down, pulled the pillows up behind her and pushed the suitcase off so he could sit down beside her.

'What does it matter?' she asked bitterly.

'Tell me, Roz.'

She read the determination in his eyes. 'There's nothing wrong with me. It's all in my mind, in other words.'

'Well, that's good news.'

She smiled ironically. 'Always assuming I can *get* into the right frame of mind, not to mention your bed . . . but perhaps I shouldn't have said that? I'm sure it could constitute an ulterior motive, *another* one . . .'

She stopped abruptly, then sat up and snapped in a furious, goaded undertone, 'Don't laugh at me, don't you dare!'

But he was, silently, and when she launched herself at him he caught her wrists and lay down with her.

'I don't understand you, I really don't,' she gasped. 'You *say* I'm not being a good wife, but when I try and change that, all you can think ... *do* ... is look for reasons to doubt it and become quite horrible. When you're not laughing at me, that is. As if—as if you expect it all to be perfect, but how can it ever be that? I'm sure even marriages made in heaven are hard to maintain in perfection without ... oh, I don't know why I bother!'

Roz stared at him, her eyes darkened to sapphire, her mouth clamped tightly shut and her breasts rising and falling visibly beneath the thin pink cotton of her blouse.

Adam returned her gaze meditatively and in a way that suddenly made a trace of pink steal into her cheeks. He said presently, 'It's a curious thing, Roz, how I like you when you're angry. I didn't know I would, or that I could make you so very angry—or that we could come to be so much at cross-purposes. Particularly over *this*,' he added significantly, and released her wrists to touch her mouth with his fingers.

'What?'

He smiled slightly. 'This ...' His fingers moved down to her chin and he tilted her head back slightly and claimed her mouth with his.

For a moment Roz was frozen with disbelief, then flooded by a determination to treat this incredibly blatant demonstration of male chauvinism with the contempt it deserved—utter passivity. Only something went strangely wrong, because in the end she found herself kissing him back, and although it was an oddly angry sort of way, it was, she realised dimly, in a more intimate way than she had ever kissed him before.

Adam lifted his head at last, but she kept her eyes closed in case he was laughing again, and flinched as he drawled softly, 'Well, well! That was a little ... surprising. Roz?'

Her lashes fluttered up and her mouth trembled. But there was no sign of amusement in his eyes, rather a dark, narrowed look as if he was trying to see through to her soul. Then she felt his fingers on the buttons of her blouse and her lips parted as he undid three or four and pushed the pink cotton aside to frame her naked breasts.

Roz put a hand to grasp his wrist, but he shook his head slightly and said quietly, 'I only want to look. It's been ...' he stopped.

'Adam ...' she breathed, and quivered down the length of her body, so close to his, so *ready*, she thought with some despair, to be helped right out of her clothes and held, slim and soft against the tall hard strength of him, to feel his weight on her, his hands in her hair or about her waist and hips, to be able to hold him and move beneath him and move her lips down his throat across his shoulder ...

Oh, where did all my anger go? she wondered as she waited motionless, because in spite of what she felt she was terribly afraid of being rejected again.

Then she was glad she had waited, although it occurred to her that it hadn't been very brave, but Adam pulled the edges of her blouse together over her breasts and said, 'Roz, it might not have been made in heaven, our marriage, but I have no intention of ending it. Have you? Seriously, I mean, and not because I provoked you this morning, for which I apologise.'

'Then,' she licked her lips, 'do you believe that I didn't encourage Nicky?' she asked huskily.

'Yes. Unfortunately it all came at me out of the blue

this morning. But have you?'

'Not really,' she whispered. 'No.'

'You have said ...'

'I know,' she interrupted. 'I ... get very confused sometimes and I guess I have thought about it, but,' she sighed, 'I've never been able to visualise it.'

'Then has it worried you that it might have been what I had in mind, despite my assurances to the contrary? No, Roz,' he pulled her a bit closer as she stirred restlessly, 'don't shy away from it. Tell me.'

She swallowed and wondered dismally what to say. Yes? But not for the reasons you think ... Could I say it?

'Yes, but Adam ...'

'Look, it's all right.' His lips twisted into a smile. 'I'd feel the same way if I thought you were determined to leave me, because despite everything, we have forged some ties between us. And because I also take some responsibility for this state of affairs.' He grimaced and smoothed her hair. 'A lot, the lion's share actually, because I had hoped to do better, make you happy, and I had hoped to make you at least feel secure and relaxed. And that's why, when it became so obvious I was only succeeding in the opposite direction, I decided we should do this. Not *this*,' he corrected with a grin. 'But *not*,' he went on, 'because I was trying to ease you out of this marriage, as you seem to think. I could find a much simpler way of doing that if I were so minded, Roz, as I think you must know. But I also gave you my word once.'

Her lashes fluttered up and down.

'Do you understand, Roz?'

'Yes. You're going to get up and ... no, Adam,' she said urgently as she saw his mouth harden, 'I do understand, really I do, and I won't make any more scenes. I'm sorry I've been so dumb about it.'

'I'm sorry I've been so horrible,' he replied with another twisted smile. 'But I came home in a bad mood and ...' He stopped rather abruptly.

'Because of me ... not understanding?' whispered Roz.

He was silent, looking past her for a moment. 'Because of something that happened to me that I didn't ... expect,' he said at last.

'While you were away?'

'Mmm.' His eyes focused back on her face.

'Could you tell me about it?' she asked diffidently.

'One day,' he said slowly. 'Perhaps ... oh hell!' he added as they heard the sound of a car driving up to the house, 'that will be Margaret and Richard. Want to come down and give me the benefit of your moral support? Unless,' he stopped as if struck by something, 'Margaret *likes* the idea of Richard and Nicky?' He looked at her searchingly.

'I don't think so,' Roz said slowly.

'You've spoken to her about it?'

'No, but she said something once, only I didn't know what she meant at the time. Now—well, once I knew what was going on a lot of little things fell into place. It was quite strange, like a kaleidoscope ... Yes,' she disengaged herself and sat up, 'I will come down, but I'll get properly dressed first. Don't ...'

'What? Lose my temper?'

She smiled faintly.

'You must be feeling better,' he said.

'... Yes.'

Adam was still lying back with a sort of lazy, twisted grace as if he was reluctant to move, and she was amazed and saddened by the clamouring impulse she felt to lie back in his arms and do what she had not had the courage to do before, but *how*? she asked herself. If there's a way I don't seem to know it.

He rolled off the bed and stood up, interrupting her curious thoughts. 'Don't be long,' he said, and rumpled her already rumpled hair with casual affection.

'No.'

The door closed on his tall figure, but she stared at it for moments with an odd kind of concentration and found herself thinking—whether she's a gorgeous geisha or whoever she is, one day I'll give you back as good as I got, Adam Milroy ... oh God, what am I thinking?

She lay back and tried to laugh at her curious obsession with geisha girls, because it was much more likely—yes, that's it, she told herself. I've got this horrible feeling it wasn't just something temporary for him. I've got this feeling he's fallen in love with someone, although he didn't believe it could happen to him. As I fell in love with *him* and didn't believe it could happen to me. But it doesn't make sense ... Unless she's not suitable to marry—perhaps she's already married? Or he *is* a man of his word ... Did they discuss it, perhaps, and did he say to her—Roz has so many problems as it is, I can't desert her, but anyway, I gave her my word?

She closed her eyes on hot tears of despair, then took a breath and whispered. 'Stop it, Roz! You're letting your imagination run wild, and all because he can do without sleeping with you for the time being, which you really only have yourself to blame for. Nor can you blame him for not understanding that your feelings have quite suddenly ... gone into reverse! But all the same, if it has happened, who could it be? I wonder ... no, surely not ... Louise? But then at the back of my mind I've always wondered about that, haven't I? If he convinced himself, when she left him, that he didn't love her, but it just wasn't true. Maybe they've met again ...?

She was lost in thought when there came the sound of another car in the driveway, but this time a glance out of the window revealed her elegant sister-in-law Lucia Whatney climbing out of her silver Alfa-Romeo with an unusually militant expression even for her on her face.

Roz grimaced and reflected that if Lucia hadn't known before, and hadn't spoken to Nicky on the phone yesterday, she certainly knew now. She turned away to get dressed hurriedly, into a cream and yellow sundress this time with matching yellow sandals, and as she put her hair up, she came to a decision.

She would do exactly as Adam wanted from now on. She would try to relax, be a friend rather than a wife, and try to banish all the hurtful speculation whirling around in her mind. After all, she thought suddenly, I may have had some mistaken ideas about this marriage and about myself, but I can still remember the pain Mrs Howard was experiencing, although she tried so hard to cover it up, and she was so ... good about her husband being attracted to me. Yet here I am putting myself through something similar.

'Anyway, I'm not achieving anything,' she whispered, 'beyond getting myself in an awful tangle.' She stood poised to leave the room and join the fray. And she stared at the bed and wondered bleakly if she'd missed the whole point.

The den was quiet and empty, but Roz soon realised why—it was too small to accommodate all the combatants. For Margaret had brought both Richard and Amy with her and Lucia must have had Flavia and Angelo with her in the car. Anyway, they were all in the lounge with Adam and Milly, and for the moment no one noticed Roz enter quietly, so she was able to take stock.

Flavia was crying into a very small white handkerchief that was mostly lace, Richard was as white as sheet and Margaret was almost as pale, but her eyes were angry instead of stunned; Lucia was in full spate and reminded Roz of Boadicea out to conquer the Romans as she raised one arm as she spoke, and Amy was starting to look tearful, while Angelo was obviously amused. Adam had his back to Roz and Milly was staring out expressionlessly over the garden.

Then Lucia paused for breath, Angelo realised Roz was there and called a greeting, whereupon everyone said Hello, Roz, with varying degrees of interest—and it was on again.

'As I was saying,' Lucia said forcefully, 'I would have expected more from you, Richard ...'

'What exactly have you got against Richard?' Margaret interrupted. 'Why don't you just come out and say that he's not *good* enough for Nicky, Lucia?'

'No, no, Lucia does not mean *that*, Margaret,' Flavia cried. 'It is not a question of that at all ...'

But Margaret continued relentlessly as if Flavia had not spoken, 'I happen to hold a different view, Lucia. It so happens I don't think Nicky's good enough for Richard. I mean this, what she's done, demonstrates that perfectly. She's an immature, spoilt *child* . . .'

'She is only a baby,' Flavia agreed.

'And I would say . . .' Lucia's eyes flashed, but Roz willed herself not to listen and wondered why Adam didn't stop it. He had turned briefly and smiled at her, then turned away again, and now as she watched his back, it struck her that he was standing very still almost as if he was waiting for something . . . Not for them to come to blows, she thought with horror, surely not?

It was Richard who stopped it. He said suddenly, '*Mother*, I'd appreciate it if you didn't speak for me as if I wasn't here. As for you, Aunt Lucia, I've behaved with the utmost propriety towards Nicky. Now I don't know what you use as a yardstick for eligibility, but I should have thought the one thing that would make me ineligible would have been that I'd taken advantage of her. I haven't done that—although I could have.'

He stopped and waited with a look of cold politeness, but for once Lucia was without words.

He turned to Adam. 'If I've made one mistake it was to try to hide it from you, Adam. But Nicky was so sure this would happen . . . However, I rang her up yesterday and told her that we couldn't go on like this any longer, that we would have to come out into the open. I also told her that you were unlikely to lock her up in a convent or send me off to fight a war, but if the family didn't approve then I would feel honour bound to wait until she was twenty-one before we married—which I'd already told her, incidentally. But I didn't know she had this in mind, because if I had, I wouldn't have allowed her to do it.

I . . .' he hesitated for the first time, 'I do know she's very young and often impetuous and it will cause us problems from time to time, but I love her for it . . . that's Nicky,' he finished.

Roz waited with bated breath, and so must everyone have been, because you could have heard a pin drop. Then she saw Adam's shoulders relax and knew immediately that he had been waiting for Richard to prove himself one way or the other.

He spoke at last. 'Richard, Roz has made a suggestion which I have to admit I was in two minds about until—about two minutes ago. Now it has my unqualified support. I see no reason why you and Nicky shouldn't become formally engaged,' Lucia and Margaret both gasped, but he ignored them, 'and if you're still both of the same mind in twelve months' time we can discuss marriage. In the meantime thank you for taking such good care of her, I'm sure it means a lot to all of us.' And he moved forward to shake Richard's hand.

Roz couldn't see Adam's expression, but she saw Richard's and had to swallow a lump in her throat.

Then, while Margaret and Lucia were still too floored to speak, while Amy stared at Adam with her mouth open and Angelo with a glint of speculation in his eyes, Flavia created a diversion. She put away her handkerchief and advanced upon Richard, stood on tiptoe and kissed him warmly. 'I didn't believe young men like you existed any more,' she said then with a twinkle in her eyes. 'So proper, so right-minded, so brave! But most importantly I think you understand Nicky, which is a very good thing. You have my blessing too!'

'Th-thank you,' said Richard, suddenly looking

rather young and bewildered. 'Thank you very much . . .'

'But it's not me you should be thanking,' Flavia interposed. 'Nor Adam, for that matter. It is Roz, because she had the wisdom to work it all out before any of us!'

'Oh!' Roz said faintly, but Richard came over to her and hugged her, which gave her a warm feeling, especially as Adam didn't seem to mind, but she did wonder how Margaret would take it.

But it seemed Richard not only had a way with Nicky, because he crossed the carpet swiftly towards his mother then and said, 'Mum, don't be angry. You told me once it was the last thing you could make to work to order, falling in love.'

Margaret's eyes softened. 'So I did,' she said, and wiped away a tear. 'Actually I feel . . . proud of you, and,' she turned to Roz, 'thank you for having faith in Richard. Not that I didn't, but,' she shrugged, 'you were unbiased.'

Roz caught her breath and glanced at Adam, but he said, 'It has to help,' and winked at her. Then he said, 'Well, shall we bend our minds to getting her back now?'

Everyone agreed except Lucia, who was looking venomously at Roz. Roz blinked and wondered why she particularly should be on the receiving end of Lucia's ire, but Milly broke the moment by saying, 'Er . . . I don't think we have to do that—bend our minds, I mean.'

Lucia transferred her green gaze to Milly and said irritably, 'Why ever not?'

But Milly merely gestured at the window and they all turned to see Nicky trudging wearily up the drive.

'My God!' breathed Adam through his teeth, but Roz

put out a hand and everyone else appeared to be numbed for a moment, then there was a general exodus to the front veranda to form a reception committee, although no one said a word.

Nicky stopped just below the veranda and looked up miserably.

It was Richard who took commmand once again. He moved forward and said sternly, 'If you ever do that again, Nicky, I'll never have anything more to do with you, I swear!'

Nicky's face crumpled like a flower. 'I won't, I won't,' she wept. 'Oh, it was so awful! My car broke down in the middle of nowhere and I had to get a lift in a lorry with no springs, which made me sick, and on top of it the driver tried to make a pass at me. I really thought I was independent enough to cope, but when you're feeling like throwing up on top of *everything* else, it's just ... Richard, don't be angry. I only did it because I love you, but you're right, we should have just come out ... have we?' she asked dazedly from the shelter of his arms now as if suddenly comprehending why almost her whole family was standing there, not to mention Richard's.

Adam said, 'Yes, Nicky, and you can thank your lucky stars it's Richard who has to deal with you, not me, because I might have been tempted to put you over my knee and spank you. However, I'll let Richard fill you in on the details and the rest of us will—oh hell, it's only half past nine in the morning! I was going to suggest a drink, but ...'

'What about a champagne breakfast?' suggested Milly. 'I could rustle one up in no time!'

'Milly, you're a genius,' said Adam with his lips quirking.

Several hours later Milly and Adam and Roz waved everyone goodbye.

The champagne breakfast had passed off well. Nicky had been absolutely radiant and Flavia, although still emotional, in a different vein altogether, which caused her to remark frequently on the sweetness of young love. Lucia had pinched her lips together, however, at every mention of it.

As for Margaret, she had taken Roz aside and confided that she only wanted Richard to be *happy*. But she had added as an afterthought that she wouldn't be surprised if Nicky found twelve months a lifetime to have to wait once she'd come down to earth.

While Angelo had approached Adam with his third glass of champagne in his hand and said, 'Seeing you don't object to *young* marriages any more, dear brother ...'

But Adam had interrupted him with a grin. 'Don't push your luck, mate! I still believe in judging each case on its merits.'

To which Angelo had replied gravely. 'I see. Ah well, perhaps I ought to start lobbying Roz in the meantime.'

Fortunately Amy had claimed Adam by then, but Lucia had overheard Angelo's last remark and directed a positively poisonous look at Roz this time.

Roz had thought, oh ... so that's it. She thinks I'm exerting too much influence. If only she knew!

But now they were waving everyone off—Nicky was going to spend the rest of the holiday with her mother—

and as both cars disappeared out of the tall gates, Milly disappeared inside and Adam exclaimed, 'Thank God they've all gone! I'm exhausted!'

Roz smiled. 'Why don't you go back to bed?'

'No. I have to go into the office for a few hours.'

'Couldn't someone come down here?' she suggested.

He shrugged. 'I guess they could, but I doubt if I'd sleep anyway. I won't be away all day. Will you . . .?' He looked at her questioningly.

'I'll be fine!' she said brightly, clinging steadfastly to her resolution, and he left about half an hour later, not noticing, as he drove off, Les approaching grimly across the lawn.

CHAPTER SEVEN

'I DON'T believe it,' said Roz dazedly.

But in the end she had to. The vet had happened to be at the stables, getting a blood sample from another horse, when Nimmitabel had got fractious, pulled away from her strapper, slipped, and been obviously lame and hopping when they caught her. He had had his portable X-ray machine with him and the X-rays had been rushed to his surgery to be developed. The result—there was no doubting that Nimmitabel had fractured the pastern bone in her left foreleg.

'So she'll never race?' said Roz, her face pale and distraught.

The vet stroked his moustache. 'Mrs Milroy, horse fractures are very difficult to deal with, as you probably know—they're so heavy, so excitable, particularly throughbreds, and prone to panic, and by nature, they spend most of their life on their feet.'

'She's . . . you're not going to have to put her down?' whispered Roz, her eyes stricken.

'*No*. Certainly not at this stage. We have techniques of dealing with this type of fracture and in the case of a valuable filly like this we'll spare no effort, but—well, even if all else goes well, as a racing proposition . . .' He stopped uncomfortably, then he said, 'I've suggested to Les that we transport her to the surgery where she can get round-the-clock expert supervision.'

'Yes. Yes . . .'

'If only Adam was here!' Les said intensely. He stared anxiously at Roz.

'It's all right, Les. He would agree, I'm sure.'

'But *you* . . .'

'I'll be fine,' she assured him. 'Just give me a few minutes with her.'

Shortly afterwards she watched the horse ambulance leave the property with Les in attendance; she turned away at last and walked unseeingly past a band of saddened stable hands.

And eventually she found herself in the same private spot where she had sat on the morning after her twenty-first birthday party and decided to try and patch up her marriage with Adam. But now, as she sat surrounded by the familiar smells, all she could think of was a foal that had for a time thought she was its mother, a filly growing strong and beautiful, a mare dying in her arms, her grandfather's dreams . . . What was left? A filly still beautiful but hobbling and in pain.

Roz closed her eyes and knew she didn't care if Nimmitabel never raced so long as she was saved, something was saved.

She sat there until the sun started to slip down and thought finally that Adam must still be out, so she got up and walked towards the house. But Adam was obviously home, because she could hear his voice in the study and guessed he was on the phone. And as she walked through the hall she heard voices in the kitchen—Jeanette and Milly. She'd forgotten Jeanette was due back and hesitated, but then she thought they all probably expected her to be still down at the stables helping with

RELUCTANT WIFE 143

the evening ritual of feeding up as she often did, and perhaps she could escape company for a little longer. So she slipped quietly upstairs and into her bedroom.

Not to know that it was Les on the phone to Adam from the veterinary clinic or that as soon as Adam finished speaking to Les, he rang the stable connection. Nor did she know that in the ensuing search it was Jeanette who thought to check the bedroom but turned away silently from the open doorway and went back downstairs just as quietly to get Adam.

Roz knew none of this as she sat on the end of her bed with her mind terribly blank and the sun started to set.

Then Adam came into the room and closed the door behind him.

Roz looked up at his tall figure, at everything about him that was so beyond her—a big, good-looking, clever man who was so much more than a match for her she couldn't for the life of her work out why he bothered...

'I'm all right,' she said, and tried to smile. 'It happens with horses, doesn't it? It's always a gamble.' She swallowed.

'Yes, Roz.'

'And they might be able to save her. That's all I care about. It's truly awful to see her like this, but...'

'Roz,' he said, 'you don't have to be so brave with me. I know how you must be feeling.'

She took a shuddering breath. 'I can cope.'

Adam came and sat down next to her and picked up her hand—and finally the tears came.

Adam let her cry, then when it seemed as if she couldn't stop he held her away from him and said, 'Roz, don't. That's enough. You'll made yourself sick.'

She took a gulp of air and scrubbed at her face distractedly, but it didn't help, and he pulled her back into arms with a frown while she clung to him, realising dimly that nothing was going to make her feel better other than to be there, pressed against his body, protected by his arms, loved . . . yes, *loved*.

'A-Adam?' she faltered. 'You've told me I have to be honest with you, haven't you?' She took several sobbing little breaths. 'I want you . . . I *need* you to make love to me now, even if it's for all the wrong reasons, but you see, I have all these lonely places in my heart and . . . and,' her tongue stumbled and she hiccuped, but the tears had slowed at last and she raised drenched blue eyes to his, 'I don't know what else to do, any more. It all—everything keeps slipping away from me . . . Would it be so hard for you?'

Adam stared down at her, his mouth set and his eyes as dark as the night.

'I'll help,' she said tremulously. 'It won't be like the other times.' She moved away, but only to slip her arms around his neck and touch her lips to the strong column of his throat.

He stayed as still as a statue. Then he said her name in a voice that made her think he was angry, but it didn't stop her. She loosened her hands behind his head and slid one beneath the open collar of his shirt while she felt for the buttons of his shirt with the other.

She said with her breath still coming erratically, 'Don't be angry, please. It's just that I feel so sad, and not only for Nimmitabel but the fool I've been. I need some reassurance—I need you.' She laid her cheek on his chest where she had opened his shirt, and although the tears had stopped, she was still shaking with emotion.

Adam said after a while, 'Roz, come with me.'

'Where? Why?'

'Into my room.' He stood up and picked her up as if she was a child. 'It's more private. No one bothers me in here.' He closed the connecting door with his heel and set her down on the bed. Then he lay down beside her and took her in his arms and held her until she was calm at last.

Then he said, 'Roz, let's get this into perspective. We ...'

But she wrenched herself free and sat up. 'No! I know what you're going to say—you're going to talk me out of it again! But I don't want to be talked to, I don't want to be reasoned with!' She glared at him, her tears forgotten. 'You seem to have forgotten about *my* conjugal rights— isn't that what you call them? Or is it only husbands who have those rights?'

A faint smile lit his eyes, but he said gravely, 'No, of course not.'

Roz thought she could kill him for laughing at her and said in a tight little voice, 'Then let's prove it.' She got awkwardly to her knees, lifted her hands behind her neck to undo the zip of her dress and pulled it defiantly over her head.

The sun was setting now and because the bedroom faced west, it was lit with a golden radiance that would soon fade to indigo shadows. But as Roz sank back on to her ankles wearing only a bra and panties, the light gilded her figure, and especially her hair which had tumbled down in drifts of curls.

She hesitated, conscious that Adam's gaze was no

longer amused and conscious of a new emotion within her that was no longer pure anger.

She took a breath and reached behind to unclip her bra, leaning forward slightly as her breasts were freed and she slid each strap off slowly. Then she folded it up carefully and put it away from her. She placed her hands on her sleek young thighs and straightened, and her high, pointed little breasts rose and fell softly in tune with her breathing. She stayed like that beneath his dark, expressionless gaze, and discovered as she waited, that from sorrow and anger, from uncertainty and defiance, she had passed on to another stage—a curious state of serenity, or perhaps to call it do or die would be more apt. But whatever, nothing could turn her back now.

'Is this doing anything for you?' she murmured, and picked up his hand. 'It is for me. Feel,' she whispered, and placed his hand over her left breast. 'Do you know what it does to me when you touch them? It sends shock waves through me right down to the tips of my toes. Do you remember when you danced with me on my birthday and you asked me what I was thinking about?'

His eyes probed her, then he nodded, the barest movement.

Her lashes fluttered and a tinge of pink stained her cheeks and throat. She said breathlessly, 'I was thinking of the last time you made love to me and how you'd kissed me here, and here.' She moved his hand. 'And just thinking of it made this happen.' She glanced down, but didn't need the evidence of her eyes to know that her nipples had unfurled like buds. 'I was shocked and terribly embarrassed,' she went on softly. 'It had never happened to me before, not in public. I felt naked and . . .

I don't know what the word is.'

The sunlight was all but gone now and the blue of her eyes seemed to be darker like the gathering shadows.

Adam said, 'Wanton?'

'Oh. Yes, that's the word,' she agreed gravely, and felt her heartbeat triple beneath his hand as she thought of it.

Perhaps he felt it too, because he sat up and for an instant Roz felt supremely vulnerable as he loomed over her. She let go of his hand and caught her bottom lip between her teeth.

'So,' he said very quietly. 'Looks can be deceiving. I would never have guessed.' And he took her by the shoulders, cupping them in his palms, then he slid his hands beneath her armpits and brushed her nipples with his thumbs. 'But it's no crime to feel like that, you know.'

Roz trembled as those long, strong hands moved round to her back and the curve of her waist, the soft flare of her bottom beneath her briefs. She closed her eyes and sighed with pleasure.

'I know,' she whispered, leaning back against his arms so that he could kiss her breasts if he wanted to. 'That was just me being the way I was. It's just as well,' her lashes swept up and she saw that he was staring at her mouth, 'it's just as well,' her lips curved into a smile and he looked up into the blue of her eyes, 'I didn't realise how much more wanton I was going to become, isn't it? Otherwise I might have locked myself away somewhere. But if you . . .'

'Roz,' Adam's dark eyes glinted and his arms tightened around her, 'there is just so much wantonness a husband can take, so don't say I didn't warn you!'

* * *

Roz woke up to the crashing symphony of a tropical thunderstorm and saw on the bedside clock that it was two-thirty in the morning. Then, as the curtains blew inwards and a fine spray of rain reached the bed, Adam stirred beside her.

'Hell,' he muttered sleepily, and got out of bed reluctantly to close the windows.

She watched him, lying perfectly still herself, and waited as he stretched, then came back to the bed and slid in beside her.

She moved to welcome him and he put his arms around her. 'Did I wake you? Sorry.'

'No. It was the storm.'

He was silent for a time with his face buried in her hair. Then he lifted his head and said, 'How do you feel?'

She opened her mouth to say fine, but paused to consider it. How did she feel?

'Wrecked,' she said softly. 'But in the nicest possible way.'

He laughed and held her close.

'How do *you* feel?' she asked.

'I shouldn't like to tell you.'

'What does that mean?' she queried, and freed a hand to smooth it along his bare shoulder.

'It means if you keep doing that, it will speak for itself shortly, my lovely Roz. However ...'

'I have great powers of recovery,' she interrupted. 'And nothing at all to do today. I could spend it like a mistress, building up my strength again, thinking about how I might tempt you tonight ...'

'I don't think I can wait that long. Tempt me now.'

She did, but it was different this time—gentle, slow, but all the same, almost unbearably lovely so she shuddered in his arms with the intensity of it. And also, like the last time, she made no attempt to hide her excitement or joy.

Afterwards, when their breathing had finally steadied and they were lying side by side holding hands, Roz turned her head and saw Adam's teeth flash in a grin.

'What?' she whispered.

'I was just thinking of ways to conserve *my* strength if this state of affairs is to continue.'

She tightened her hand around his suddenly. 'Don't you want it to?'

He turned towards her and kissd her cheek. 'Of course I do, Roz.'

'Then you're not ... angry with me?'

'Does it look like it? *Feel* like it?'

'No,' she said slowly. 'But wasn't *your* idea the oppposite? And when you get up, I mean, in the cold hard light of day ...'

'I've already been up,' he broke in. 'Not in the cold hard light of day but earlier, after the first time. When you fell asleep I found I couldn't. So I got up and ... reassured our household among other things,' he said drily.

'Oh ...'

'But I came back, Roz.'

There was silence. Then she relaxed with a sigh and buried her head in his shoulder. And she thought, that's what matters, I can live with that. To expect him to say he loves me is asking for the moon, but that he wanted to come back, isn't angry—that's enough for me.

* * *

To live in acknowledged intimacy with a man was quite different, Roz discovered, from what had passed before in her marriage to Adam. It was also apparently evident to quite a lot of people that something had changed.

Jeanette for example, seemed to sense it immediately.

'Oh, I've misssed you!' Roz said warmly. She was in her own bed at Adam's suggestion and wearing her white silk pyjamas, and Jeanette had arrived bearing breakfast on a tray—again at Adam's suggestion, Roz guessed. He had gone to see Nimmitabel. 'Did you have a good time?'

'Super,' Jeanette said enthusiastically. 'But I'm glad to be back.' Her round face sobered. 'I was so sorry to hear about the filly, though. Do you . . . I mean yesterday . . .' She stopped.

Roz looked down at the tray and her hair shadowed her face. Then she looked up and smiled. 'I was terribly upset yesterday, but that's not going to help. Anyway, Adam's gone to see her now.'

'He'll know what's best for her,' Jeanette said confidently, and surprised herself by adding, 'Like he did for you.' She studied Roz candidly, though.

Roz's eyes widened slightly.

'I mean—well, you look so calm and beautiful this morning,' Jeanette said seriously. 'Only Mr Milroy could have done that for you.'

How ironic! Roz thought. If Jeanette knew the length I had to go to to persuade Mr Milroy . . . but then the final irony is that she's right. Only Mr Milroy could have. She felt her cheeks reddening at the thought, but Jeanette was looking around the bedroom as if checking out her domain and seeing how it had fared during her absence.

Roz grimaced inwardly as she thought of the havoc she'd wreaked in her bureau drawers yesterday—was it only yesterday?

Milly was another one who sensed a different aura about Roz very soon, but being Milly, she forbore to comment.

Adam came home at lunchtime and found Roz in the den. He took her into his arms and kissed her lingeringly, then sat down with her in his lap.

'How is she?' she asked.

'I think she's going to make it,' he said meditatively. 'She's somewhat sedated most of the time, but between times she's behaving pretty sensibly, for her.'

'Perhaps she's . . . grown up overnight,' Roz suggested.

He smiled slightly. 'Perhaps.'

'To race, do you think, Adam?'

He took his time answering. 'There've been so many miracles associated with her, Roz . . . but no, I doubt it.'

'It doesn't matter. So long as they can save her.' She stirred in his arms. 'When can I see her?'

'Leave it for a couple of days,' he advised. 'She's getting the best attention possible and it's vital that they get her to settle.'

'I wouldn't upset her,' promised Roz.

'I know, but you might upset yourself. Nothing's going to happen to her in the meantime.'

'All right,' Roz said obediently. 'What are you going to do for the rest of the day? Go to work?'

'No, I'm going to play hooky,' he said seriously.

'Oh?'

'Mmm. For the next couple of days, as a matter of fact. I'm going to book into the Ramada, spend some time lazing on the beach, dine out every evening, possibly go to the casino and spend the rest of the time in bed.'

'Alone?'

'Very much so,' he said with a glint in his dark eyes as they rested on her upturned, slightly wary face. 'Alone with you.'

Some time later she said, 'In that case I ought to go and pack.'

'Jeanette's doing it. Talking of which, they tell me my luggage should arrive tomorrow. There's a surprise . . .' Adam stopped suddenly, '. . . for you in it,' he finished on an oddly dry note.

Are you going to tell me or do I have to wait?' teased Roz.

'Wait.'

'Not even a clue?'

'No, except—well, I could say I had no idea how appropriate it would be.' And almost as if he was changing the subject Adam said then, 'How are all the lonely places of your heart now, Roz?'

'F-filled,' she said unsteadily, and turned her face into his shoulder. With love, she longed to add but didn't.

Adam made no further mention of those matters over the next magical days, although Roz did catch him watching her with a curious intensity several times, which she found disturbing but decided to ignore. But she thought, of course he must be wondering why I changed so drastically. Will he guess one day that I was fighting for my life, that I *was* desperately afraid of losing him? Will he one day understand why?

They went to the casino on their last night.

Not long open and the first casino in Queensland, although a second was taking shape in Townsville, Jupiter's Casino on the Gold Coast had attracted enormous attention. The building alone was spectacular, situated on an island in the Nerang River behind Broadbeach and including a Conrad International hotel, restaurants, convention facilities and of course, beneath a sloping glass roof that at night became a river of light, the two glittering floors of the casino itself.

Dress was flexible, as was the custom in Queensland, but Roz wore a sleeveless black voile dress with a gathered skirt and a silky polyester lining that hugged her breasts and left the golden skin above, bare beneath the round-necked shadowy voile of the bodice. With it she wore high, open-toed black sandals and her only jewellery was her diamond-studded gold bracelet. She left her hair loose and the black accentuated her fairness.

'Too dressy?' she asked Adam, after taking quite some time because even dressing, especially in something like this, seemed to have acquired a sensuous pleasure of its own these days.

'No. And we can always hock the bracelet if we lose,' he said with a grin. 'Don't stray far away from me tonight, will you, Roz?'

'No. Why not?'

'Someone might be tempted to kidnap you.'

Her eyes widened. 'Because of the bracelet?'

'Because you look so desirable.'

'Oh,' she relaxed. 'I doubt it. It could be the other way round,' she added with a glint of laughter in her blue eyes.

'And what,' he strolled over to her and put a finger on

the point of her chin, 'do you mean by that, my little witch?'

Roz pretended to consider and put up a hand to stroke his immaculate burgundy linen open-necked shirt. 'Some,' she paused, 'exotic lady might be tempted to lure you away.'

'Oh,' he said softly, 'she'd have to be very exotic to compete with you, Roz.'

Roz blushed, knowing exactly what he was referring to, and laughed. 'You must think—one day I'll explain that to you. Can we go? I'm dying to win a fortune!'

She turned away to pick up her purse, and that was one of the occasions when she turned back, to find him watching her intently. But she pretended not to notice.

'Adam! I don't believe it,' she exclaimed later, counting a pile of chips. 'I'm exactly back to where I started!'

They were having a drink and a midnight snack in the Garden Restaurant, and she was flushed and excited.

'That's a very creditable performance,' he drawled. 'I wish I could say the same.'

'You haven't lost much, though.'

'No,' he agreed. 'I must be too cautious by nature.'

'You must be,' she said thoughtfully. 'I mean, you never lose your head at the races, or your shirt.' She grimaced.

'I learnt that lesson a long time ago, Roz. And I don't see racing as a gambling medium so much as a . . . as an industry which I happen to enjoy being involved in. As for this,' he lifted a hand expressively, 'it's fun once in a while, but deadly if you imagine you can beat the house in the long term.'

Roz pushed her plate away and wiped her lips. 'I didn't think I would enjoy it so much,' she confessed. 'Perhaps I did inherit some of my grandfather's failings, after all.'

'To enjoy yourself for an evening is no crime, Roz. In fact I was going to suggest one more fling before we go. What's it to be? Two-up? Roulette?'

'Blackjack,' she said positively. 'I told you I was a pontoon player from way back, didn't I?'

Roz was amazed to discover that although it was a week night and after midnight, there still seemed to be as many people as ever around the tables and the two-up ring with its plush, salmon pink carpet, the centre of a lively crowd drawn by a run of 'heads'.

But Adam found her a seat at a Blackjack table, the girl croupier smiled at her and dealt her in, and for some minutes she became absorbed in the game. Then she looked around for Adam, to see he was not far away, in deep conversation with an elderly man she didn't recognise. But all evening people had stopped to talk to them, many she hadn't known. Adam lifted a hand as he caught her gaze and she turned back to the table with a smile.

Then she became aware of the woman sitting at the other end of the table. She must have slipped into an empty seat while Roz had had her head turned away, and if Roz had been asked to describe the exotic lady she had mentioned earlier to Adam, it crossed her mind that this gorgeous creature would fit the bill perfectly.

She looked to be in her early thirties, tall with long golden-blonde hair and green-flecked eyes, and she was wearing a low cut, green silk dress held up over a magnificent bosom by narrow shoulder straps. And as she scratched the table for another card an enormous square cut emerald ring surrounded by diamonds caught the light.

But the card she got gave her more than twenty-one, and she turned with a wry little smile to a man standing behind her and he fondly slipped a hundred-dollar bill into her hand which she handed to the croupier to be changed into chips.

That was when she looked idly across at Roz, her lovely hazel eyes widened and her gaze lifted, and Roz felt Adam's hand on her shoulder.

But when Roz twisted to smile up at him, he wasn't looking down at her but across the table, with his mouth hardening. Roz felt her own eyes widen as she turned back, because it was the woman in green he was staring at, she realised, but it was more, it was as if there was an electrically charged current flowing across the green baize table top between them which seemed to touch everyone around them, even the croupier, who turned her head from one to the other and blinked a couple of times before she returned to cutting a pack of cards.

Then that green-flecked gaze slid down to study Roz thoroughly, and for some reason she caught her breath and felt Adam's hand tighten on her shoulder. She couldn't tear her eyes away.

Until the croupier called, 'Place your bets, please,' and the woman in green smiled faintly and did the strangest thing. She raised one hand to sketch a salute, then turned to the table.

Adam said a moment later, 'Had enough, Roz?'
'Yes. Yes!'

* * *

They lay side by side high above the Paradise Centre in their room in the luxurious new Ramada Hotel, not speaking, not sleeping.

Adam had been quiet on the way back from the casino and Roz the same, still gripped by that curious encounter.

He had already been in bed when Roz came out of the bathroom, lying with his hands behind his head, and he hadn't stirred as she moved quietly about the room, tidying up. Then she had slipped beneath the sheet beside him and he had slid an arm around her shoulder but not turned his head.

She moved closer now and laid her cheek on his shoulder. 'Who was she?'

He said, when she thought he wasn't going to answer, 'Louise.'

'I wondered if that was who she was,' Roz murmured. 'She's very beautiful and unusual.'

'So are man-eating tigers, I'm told,' he said drily.

'Is this,' Roz hesitated, 'the first time you've seen her since . . .'

'Yes. They live in Perth.'

She asked no more questions, and presently he gathered her into his arms and as they lay together she felt the tension drain out of him. 'I thought,' Adam said into her hair, 'rather, I used to think what a triumph it would be to see her again, to be able to show her that I'd made it—show her what she'd walked away from.'

'And it wasn't like that?' Roz asked gently.

'No. The opposite. It was her moment of triumph. Which made me angry, I guess. Because all these years

I've avoided looking one fact in the face.'

Roz held her breath.

'I might not have loved her,' he explained, 'but she dented my pride pretty badly. And all this time I've thought of her as grasping and on the make, deep down. I've thought . . . all right, even if I fell out of love with her, or perhaps I was never *in* love with her, I didn't do *that* to her—walk away into the arms of another woman. But she's proved me wrong. And in doing so, exposed my ego.'

'Do you mean . . .?'

'I think I mean it would have been all right if I'd sent her away, but to be walked out on, and for another man who was richer and older, rather stuck in my gullet. Which is ridiculous, because the alternative was to live together in misery. I *knew* that—pride is a crazy thing, obviously.'

'But she's stuck to him?' Roz whispered.

'Yes. And made him very happy, I would say, by the look of it.'

'Do you think she fell in love with him, or . . .?'

'I don't know, Roz. Not at the time, I didn't. Now it doesn't seem to matter. What matters is that she had the perception and wisdom to take her life into her own hands. I believe they have four children.'

Roz winced. 'And I have you,' Adam said very quietly, and began to make love to her with exquisite slowness.

They left on Sunday morning quite early. But as they were waiting to turn on to the highway, who should walk across their bows but none other than Michael Howard and a girl of about twenty.

Roz blinked and stared.

They were holding hands, Mike and his wife, and she was unexceptionally pretty and had quality Roz couldn't for an instant put her finger on. Then it occurred to her, as they walked on down the pavement on her side of the car, that she looked practical and capable, somehow—like Mrs Howard.

She watched them as Adam drew out into the traffic, which was heavy, so for a time they kept pace. They were talking, engrossed in each other and, it was easy to see, happy. And for Roz it was like watching an acquaintance, not someone who once had desperately wanted to marry her.

Then they turned a corner and she turned to Adam. He took his eyes of the road and there was a query in them.

'What a coincidence,' she said a little breathlessly. 'I mean, you seeing Louise the other day and me seeing Mike today.'

He didn't say anything, but when they stopped at a traffic light, he put his hand over hers.

'How did you know about him? Being married?' she asked.

'He applied for a job with us—not Milroy Electronics but a subsidiary company. He probably didn't realise it was connected. I happened to be attending a managerial conference when his application came up for consideration. All his particulars were on the form, and because the name rang a bell, I looked at it. They're living with his parents—that was the address he gave, anyway—and his wife is a nurse. They've been married for about four months now.'

'Did you . . .?' she hesitated.

'I didn't intervene one way or the other. But they were looking for someone more experienced.'

'I ...' She started again. 'It was like looking at a stranger and it all seems so far away now. His father must approve ... of her.'

Adam began, 'Roz ...' then swore as a car loomed up beside them and with no warning whatsoever ducked in front of them so that he had to jam his brakes on to avoid hitting it. But they themselves were jolted forward then as the car behind ran into the back of the Jaguar.

To add to the confusion, a highway patrol car lurking in a side street must have witnessed the whole incident, because it cut on to the highway with lights flashing and siren blaring in pursuit of the car which had caused it all.

Roz swallowed and went pale.

'Are you all right?' demanded Adam, his face pale too but furious.

'Yes,' she said shakily.

'You don't look it.'

'I'm fine. I just got a fright, and then that ... siren.'

He swore again and put an arm around her. 'Relax,' he ordered. 'I doubt if anyone's hurt.' He got out.

No one was, and the damage to the rear of the Jaguar was less than to the bonnet of the car behind. Presently a highway patrolman on a motorbike rode up and spoke to Adam and the other driver and took particulars, then dealt with the snarl-up in the traffic.

'A carload of young hoons,' said Adam, getting back in, and adding disgustedly, 'Drunk—at this time of the morning! They were spotted further back, but because of the traffic, instead of chasing them the police radioed ahead.'

'Did they catch them?'

'Yes—fortunately before they did any more damage. Well,' he started the car and listened attentively, but it sounded as smooth as ever, 'we're mobile at least, which is more than the poor beggars behind are, so let's get home and out of this. Feeling better?'

'Yes.'

'Sure?'

'Yes. Yes, I am,' Roz said with decision. 'I can't spend the rest of my life going into shock every time I hear a siren, can I?' And she smiled at him genuinely.

He narrowed his eyes briefly, another curious look, but it was so fleeting, she didn't have to take evasive action. And he said with a grin, 'No, ma'am.'

CHAPTER EIGHT

LIFE at home was calm and restful for a time after their brief holiday. Restful for Roz at least, but Adam spent a lot of time away from home and at other times was unusually preoccupied. Roz pondered this, but, although with a niggle of doubt sometimes, attributed it to the Japanese agency he had acquired. Anyway, she had decided to take her life into her own hands with wisdom and perception and always banished those doubts resolutely.

After all, she told herself, she had great cause for hope, hadn't she? She might not have been able to tell him in so many words that she loved him, but she'd fought for and won the right to show him. And two of the outstanding problems of their relationship had been vanquished, she felt. He had really come to terms with his first marriage—and that must diminish his cynicism about falling in love, and perhaps women in general now that he could admire and respect Louise, she reasoned. While for her the spectre of both Louise and Mike Howard had been laid for ever, for Adam too, she hoped and prayed.

And when the startling thought popped into her mind one day that the fact that it wasn't Louise she had to worry about didn't mean it couldn't be another woman, nor was it unknown for men to be quite happily polygamous, she immediately felt ashamed and as if she was maligning Adam. And more convinced than ever of the unwisdom of indulging in futile speculation.

Something else that puzzled her, though, she did allow herself to think about freely. Adam had said he'd brought back a surprise from Tokyo, but although she knew his lost luggage had finally turned up he had made no further mention of the surprise. Perhaps *it* hasn't turned up yet, though, she mused. Perhaps it was a separate item. And perhaps it's silly not to just ask him outright, but I don't seem to be able to do that. He did sound a bit strange when he mentioned it, didn't he? I wonder why . . .

Several antidotes for her suppressed and acknowledged concerns helped greatly, however. She discovered during the peace of those weeks a feeling of more interest in her home and a desire to be more involved in running it. This first came about when she mentioned out of the blue to Milly that she had always been interested in herbs and would like to start a garden of them and perhaps use more herbs in their cuisine. She had broken off then to apologise rather disjointedly in case Milly thought she was being critical.

But Milly, it seemed, had been waiting for the day Roz would take more interest in the household, because she said, 'What a great idea! We could make teas—all sorts of things. By the way, I was going to mention that the wallpaper and the seat coverings in the dining-room look a little shabby, which is a good excuse for doing some redecorating in there. I usually get an interior decorator in, but would you . . .?'

Roz would love to, she decided. Then Nimmitabel passed the crucial period and the fracture was pronounced to be healing well—well enough for her to be put to stud eventually and spend the rest of her days pursuing maternity. Like me, thought Roz with some irony. I hope she's more successful!

Two weeks later, the herb garden had been dug and planted and the dining-room redecorated. The speed with which they had been able to finish the dining-room was mostly due to Jeanette, who had proved a dab hand at upholstery, and now the twelve magnificent mahogany chairs had dull yellow slub silk seat covers which matched the wallpaper, although they had got a professional in to hang that.

It was Flavia, calling in unexpectedly, who helped Roz to add the finishing touches.

'My dear Roz,' she cried as she stared round the all but finished room, 'I adore it! I had no idea you were so gifted.'

Roz smiled ruefully, then sobered. 'It needs a few—I'm not quite sure *what*—to finish it off, though. None of the ornaments or lamps we had before seem to fit. I *thought* all white perhaps, but . . .' She shrugged.

Flavia blinked, then said softly, 'But how perfect . . . perhaps with just one focal touch of a soft jade green. Come with me, Roz!' she commanded. 'I know just where to go.'

Hours later Roz arrived back from an arduous tour of all Flavia's favourite antique shops exhausted but happy, as she explained to Adam that night when she took him into the dining-room and described what they had bought. 'I think the alabaster lamps will look super on the sideboard, and we found this enormous pottery vase with a beautiful soft green glaze and perfectly elegant handles at the neck that could stand here, and then a really unusual ceramic candelabrum for the table. That's all . . . oh no, we got a new dinner service and some table linen,' she remembered guiltily. 'I've spent an awful lot of your money today, Adam.'

'Egged on by my mother, no doubt,' he commented.

'She . . . well, she did say she was sure you wouldn't mind.'

'That sounds like her,' he said a shade drily.

Roz hesitated and felt her cheeks grow warm. 'Do you mind? Perhaps I should have checked with you first. Only she arrived out of the blue today and . . . we did have fun,' she finished lamely.

'That sounds like my mother too. By the way,' he idly examined the colour in her cheeks, 'you don't have to look like a naughty schoolgirl. I'm not going to beat you for having so much fun!'

Roz's expression changed to one of indignation. 'You were teasing me!'

'I just couldn't resist it,' he murmured. 'And now I'm going to kiss you. Any objection? After all, you said yourself you'd spent an awful lot of my money today.'

'Well . . . but I saved you some too. Milly was going to get a decorator in, so we didn't have *that* expense, and Jeanette made the seat covers. And your mother drives a mean bargain with antique dealers, believe me, whereas a decorator . . . Adam,' she protested breathlessly, 'Not here!'

His long fingers stilled on the front of her blouse. 'You had somewhere else in mind?' he asked, his dark eyes glinting wickedly.

'No! Dinner will be ready soon . . .'

'But you said not *here*, which made me think you had

somewhere else in mind, like your bedroom. I'm easy.' His fingers moved on her buttons again until her blouse was open to the waistband of her skirt and he slipped his hands inside to cup her breasts. She'd showered after coming home and not bothered to put a bra on because it was a hot, still evening.

'Oh,' she whispered, 'I think you're in an impossible mood. You *know* what I meant . . . Someone could come in at any moment!'

'Why? We don't use this room when we're on our own. Anyway, do you care?' said Adam softly. 'They'd only turn around and go straight out again.'

Roz stared up at him, her lips parted and her lashes fluttering as he drew his thumbs across her nipples. She trembled beneath his hands and felt her control slipping. She tore her gaze away and looked around a little wildly—at the smooth, bare surface of the dining-room table—and gasped at the images that flooded her mind.

He followed her gaze, and when she looked back at him he had one eyebrow raised and a wicked smile playing on his lips. 'Roz . . .'

'Don't,' she begged, and convulsively buried her head in his chest. 'Don't *tease* me!'

Adam withdrew his hands and put his arms around her and she could feel him laughing. 'It's not *funny*,' she said tensely, and thought she must be blushing from head to toe, so hot did she feel, and not only because of her incredible thoughts but because he had understood immediately.

'Perhaps not,' he said after a moment, 'but wildly imaginative and . . . innovative,' he added barely audibly.

Roz groaned. 'Oh . . . it was *you*! I might . . . I might never be able to come *in* here again, let alone give a dinner party . . . oh!'

But when he stopped laughing this time, and resisting her efforts to free herself, he said, 'That would be a pity after all your hard work. And I shall very much enjoy coming in here again, and entertaining in here, because we'll be able to share a very private joke, won't we, my lovely, unexpectedly naughty but fascinating Roz?'

She caught her breath and forced herself to look up at him at last.

'Roz, don't look like that. I'm sorry,' he said with returning gravity.

Her lips quivered, then suddenly she was giggling helplessly, but there was a tap on the door then and she froze and thanked God she had her back to it, while Adam pressed her closer to him as Jeanette said,

'Dinner is served, Mr Milroy . . . oh! Sorry! I didn't mean . . .'

'That's all right, Jeanette,' Adam said calmly over Roz's head. 'We'll be there in a minute.'

'Well, there's no hurry. I'm sure Milly could . . . I mean . . .'

'Don't bother, Jeanette,' said Adam seriously, but Roz could feel the effort it cost him, while Jeanette apparently took the hint, because Roz heard her walk away.

'I told you!' she whispered. 'Now I haven't only to face this room again, but them.' She was laughing, though, and as he released her and carefully did up her buttons they laughed quietly together, although he did have the grace to look rather rueful.

'There—all proper and prudent again,' he murmured, and kissed her lips. 'And I'll help you face them.' He took her hand.

But later that evening he was preoccupied again, and although he came to her bed, there was something restrained about his lovemaking, as if he had been dwelling on something that had doused their earlier encounter.

Roz was pondering it all the next morning as she unpacked her new treasures which had arrived in an early delivery.

She decided to set the table with the new linen and dinner service, just to see how it looked, and they were all three, she and Milly and Jeanette, admiring it when Lucia arrived.

'Well, well,' observed Lucia as Milly, who had gone to answer the door, ushered her into the dining-room, 'Mother said you and she had gone on a shopping spree, Roz.' She looked around critically. 'Quite nice,' she murmured.

Milly, who was standing behind her, raised her eyes heavenwards fleetingly but said, 'I was just going to make Mrs Milroy some coffee, Mrs Whatney. Would you care for some?'

'Thank you, Milly,' said Lucia.

'We'll have it in the den, please, Milly,' Roz requested. 'Come through, Lucia. This is a . . . surprise.'

Lucia smiled a faint, cool smile, and Roz was reminded of the last time she had seen her sister-in-law on the fateful morning Nicky had tried to run away, and she recalled the venomous green glances she had been on the receiving end of and the sudden conviction she had had that Lucia had bitterly resented her intervention on Richard and Nicky's behalf. It occurred to her that Lucia might also resent her shopping spree with Flavia—or at least, what it represented—a closer relationship with Flavia.

But for about half an hour they drank their coffee and sampled the cook's special melt-in-the-mouth shortbread and chatted quite amiably about nothing in particular.

Then Lucia asked abruptly, 'How's Adam?'

'Fine. He's in Sydney but due home tomorrow. Why ... I mean, why do you ask?'

Lucia shrugged. 'Oh, I just wondered. I must say you cope with it all very well, Roz. But then I did realise quite some time ago that yours was a ... rather *different* marriage.'

Roz blinked. 'What do you mean?'

'Don't get me wrong!' Lucia waved an elegantly manicured hand. 'I'm all in favour of businesslike marriages. Although I did expect Adam to be ... well, more discreet about it. But you seem to be able to handle that, so ...' She stopped and glanced at Roz's dazed, uncomprehending face. 'Do you mean you didn't know that he took his mistress to Japan with him? My dear, I happened to have a close friend who was on the same flight, and they were not only together on the flight but together at the hotel in Tokyo! And she—this friend of mine—later happened to see him buying this gorgeous, fabulously expensive kimono for her the night after,' she paused, then went on significantly, 'she'd seen him coming out of her bedroom. Their ... er ... affair was rather well publicised some years ago, but of course

Adam would never have married her.'

'Why not?' Roz heard herself saying as if from a great distance.

'She's been divorced twice, she's a career woman and I've personally heard her say she's not interested in giving up her career to raise children. I expect this ... new arrangement they have now suits them both very well.'

Roz licked her lips. 'And what ...' She stopped and started again. 'And what gave you the idea that our marriage was so different, Lucia? Apart from this ...'

Lucia smiled. 'You did, Roz. I've seen enough young girls in love to know that you weren't. Was I wrong?' she asked indulgently.

'No ... But I am now ...' Oh God, did I say that? Roz wondered frantically. Yes ... She put a hand to her lips and stared at Lucia and thought, how *could* you ... how could you *do* this to anyone? What business of yours is it anyway, *whatever*, even if you are right, were right ... what have I ever done to you? And now you've made me bare my soul to you ...

'Well,' said Lucia, 'that's unfortunate.'

'Lucia!' Roz gasped at the wave of anger that overcame her, but without it she would never have been able to say what she did. 'Don't think I don't know why you've chosen to tell me all this. For some reason you resent me having any influence in this family, yet it's the last thing I want or seek.'

'Oh? What about Nicky?'

'What happened with Nicky was entirely coincidental—how I came to be involved in it, at least!'

'Tell me about it,' Lucia said tauntingly.

'No. It's between me and Adam, and that's the way it's going to stay. But if you're jealous that I might be somehow upstaging you in this family, you're wasting time and petty emotion, and I can't believe that anyone could be so ... so *pretentious* and ridiculous!'

Lucia narrowed her green eyes. 'And you don't think it's pretentious, Roz, to be queening it among us when you're no better off than I am ...' She stopped and her face paled, then to Roz's utter amazement, it crumpled and she put up a hand, then turned away abruptly, but beneath the elegant lines of her saffron suit, Roz could see that her shoulders were shaking.

'Lucia ...?'

No response.

Roz tried again, then went down on her knees beside her distraught sister-in-law's chair. 'Please—I don't understand,' she said huskily. 'Don't cry so ... let me help. You said ...' She broke off and her eyes widened. 'Do you mean you and Gareth——?'

Lucia huddled lower in her chair, looking boneless and pathetic in a way Roz would never have dreamt possible.

'Does he ... is he ...?'

'Yes,' Lucia wept. 'He's been unfaithful to me for years, and it's killing me slowly, because I love him and I hate him and I could never leave him ...'

It all came out, a litany of misery that for years, Roz guessed, Lucia had barricaded within her heart and camouflaged beneath her naturally somewhat abrasive personality. But the price she had paid had been to watch herself growing more waspish, even shrewish ...

'I just can't seem to help myself—sometimes I hate myself even more than I hate Gareth, only of course I don't hate him. I . . . I tremble like a foolish girl every time another affair is over and he wants me again. I fall in love all over again, I . . . *why*,' she went on with bitter, tearful intensity, 'can't I either leave him or accept that that's the kind of man he is and be content that he's happy to stay married to *me*, even though he strays and probably always will. Why do I torment myself and tear myself apart like this every time it happens, and . . . and torment anyone else who happens to be within reach?'

What can I say? Roz thought, and said nothing. But she put her hand over Lucia's and held it.

They sat like that for a long time until Lucia had quietened at last. Then she said, 'It seems we are in the same boat, so perhaps we could help each other.'

'Oh, Roz,' Lucia said miserably. 'I'll never forgive myself for this, especially if you didn't know.'

'There's . . . there's no chance of it being wrong—your friend, I mean?'

'She's never been wrong about Gareth,' Lucia said with irony, then closed her eyes briefly and bit her lip. 'But perhaps it was just an interlude for Adam,' she said then. 'Just something that happened when they found themselves in Tokyo together, and alone. In fact there's nothing to suggest otherwise,' she said almost eagerly. 'What *I* said about her being his mistress was only . . . sort of conjured up because . . . because . . .' She took an unsteady breath. 'Because of my paranoia. And that's *true*, Roz.'

And that's *true*, Roz . . .

For some reason for the rest of the day, those particular words of Lucia's stayed in Roz's mind like a refrain.

She had stayed to lunch, and by the time she left, the only indication that she might not be her normal self was that she was a bit pale. Unless you looked closely into her eyes, which Roz did, and saw the guilt and the anxiety. But, as Roz had said to her, it's an ill wind, and at least we understand each other now, and can be friends.

And that, she thought, as she watched the silver Alfa-Romeo drive away, is something of a miracle, because if anyone had told me I would one day achieve this kind of rapport with Lucia Whatney, I wouldn't have believe it. And that's *true*, Roz.

But before she turned to go back inside, she took a deep breath and concentrated carefully on how to project a carefree image to Milly and Jeanette, both of whom would be curious about the visit anyway.

It wasn't until she was getting ready for bed that night that it occurred to her that she had put her heart and soul into allaying any suspicions Milly and Jeanette might have had to stop herself thinking about Adam. And had been highly successful—on both fronts. Except for those four words of Lucia's she had so stupidly got on the brain.

But you can't not think about it for ever, Roz, she told herself as she showered and changed. For example, didn't he *say* that something had happened to him in Tokyo, something unexpected? And he didn't actually deny it when I asked him if there was someone else. Is he really in Sydney on business?

She climbed into bed, the bed where Adam had made love to her so restrainedly the night before, and that was when the clinical numbness that seemed to have her mind in its grip faded, and she found herself hugging a pillow, dry-eyed but battered by so many emotions at last, the uppermost one disbelief. Even if it had happened in Tokyo, surely the way they were now meant there couldn't be another woman in his life? But, the thought kept creeping in, the way they were now hadn't been what Adam had planned for them, had it? She had almost forced it on him, and in the end, perhaps it had only been an act of kindness on his part. Poor Roz... she flinched. Poor lonely Roz.

And with that, belief came crowding in. Adam had been different, hadn't he? In between times. But she'd closed her mind to it. Now she could only understand why. While she might be receiving his comfort and support, another woman had his heart, because despite Lucia's attempts to lay the spectre of a permanent relationship, didn't it all fit in with what had happened since her twenty-first birthday? Yes...

Then, as the night wore on, came the thoughts she was to think of as the bottom line. What to do? Pretend she didn't know? Be torn apart like Lucia? Was it worse or better to know there was only one other woman in your husband's life rather than a succession of them? Worse, she decided. Because it meant he must love her.

Roz woke the next morning with nothing resolved in her mind and the knowledge that Adam would be home that night.

But one source of consolation was that she unexpectedly found herself alone during the day. It was Milly's day off, but Jeanette, who had been looking somewhat subdued for a couple of days, finally broke down and admitted that she had toothache but hated going to the dentist.

Roz dosed her with aspirin and packed her off to her own dentist with stern admonitions not to return if she chickened out, then commanded her to spend the afternoon with her mother.

The pain must have got the upper hand, because Jeanette went like a lamb.

But the relief Roz felt at not having to act a part any longer was tempered by a sense of miserable confusion and intolerable sadness. She just didn't know what to do next, and no amount of thinking about it seemed to help.

She finally wandered out to her new herb garden, observed that the weeds were growing a lot faster than the herbs and set out to get rid of them.

Half an hour later, hot and grubby, she glanced up suddenly, for no reason other than a suddenly uncomfortable feeling, to see Adam standing there watching her.

She gasped. 'Adam! I didn't hear you! Have you been home long?' She scrambled up off her knees and pushed a strand of hair off her face, leaving a steak of dirt on her cheek.

He moved. 'No—about five minutes. You were obviously engrossed.'

'Yes. Yes, I was.' She stripped off her gloves and brushed her white shorts and tucked in the back of her sky blue T-shirt. 'I also wasn't expecting you until this evening, but I'm not complaining. Isn't it *hot*! Come in and I'll make us something cool to drink. How was Sydney?' she asked brightly.

Adam didn't reply immediately, just watched her shake out the mat she'd been kneeling on and wrap her tools up in it, then hesitate for a fleeting instant before she walked towards him and tilted her face up for his kiss.

Then he said, 'Sydney was cold. How are you?' and kissed her briefly.

'Fine!' she heard herself say gaily.

'Where is everyone?'

Roz explained as she led the way into the kitchen and chatted on about heaven knew what as she washed her hands at the sink, then mixed a jug of lime squash and asked if he was hungry.

Again he took his time about replying, and as he stood watching her, leaning his shoulders against the wall, she was able to think that he looked tired but that there was something else in his dark eyes that she couldn't fathom, something that frightened her and spurred her to further small talk when he finally said no, he wasn't hungry.

'Let's go into the den and be comfortable. It's not often that we have the place all to ourselves, is it?'

The ceiling fan was on in the den, but Adam discarded the jacket of his beautiful lightweight grey suit and pulled off his navy blue tie before saying, 'No, we don't. Nor could their timing be better in this instance.'

Roz put their drinks down and said lightly, 'Is something wrong? Would you rather have had a beer? I didn't think of that . . .' But at last she was able to get a grip on herself, because of course something was wrong—he had come to a decision. She put a hand briefly to her mouth and forced herself to look across at him and to say quietly, 'Sorry. What is it?'

'I thought you might like to tell me that. At least I did think that, but you appear to be perfectly normal, happy and bright, in fact.' He looked at her sardonically.

'Adam . . . I don't understand,' she whispered.

'You don't do you, Roz? You honestly don't. Well, I'll tell you.' He strolled over to her and took her chin in his fingrs, while she stared up at him, her eyes wide and dark. 'When I got back from Sydney this morning, earlier than anticipated, I went straight to the office, where there was a message for me. An urgent message,' he added softly, but a shiver went down her spine, 'to contact my beloved sister Lucia.'

Her lips parted and her eyes were dazed, then stunned. 'She . . .' she licked her lips, 'she *told* you?'

'Mmm . . . About all the things she'd told *you*, Roz. Didn't you believe her?'

'I . . .' A tide of hot colour stole into Roz's cheeks and she couldn't go on.

'She was right, you know,' he said. 'I did find myself next to an old flame on the flight to Tokyo, I did leave her hotel room at an ungodly hour, I did purchase a kimono in her presence.'

'Oh, Adam!' breathed Roz. 'I . . .'

'But apparently you didn't mind finding all that out, Roz,' he overrode her roughly. 'You were prepared to go on as if nothing had happened. Indeed,' he traced the outline of her mouth with one finger. 'It wasn't an earth-shattering event for you at all. And of course I know why,' he told her with devastating irony.

'Do you?' her voice wasn't working too well and the words came out huskily.

He smiled, the coolest smile she'd ever seen. 'So long as you can keep all this you don't really care what I do behind your back.'

Roz pulled free. 'I gather you didn't discuss that with Lucia?'

His mouth hardened and a flash of brilliant anger lit his eyes. '*No*. It was quite a brief conversation, actually, and the last we'll be having for some time. Just as this is the last conversation you and I will be having, Roz. You see, I'm no longer content to be just a stopgap for all the lonely places of your heart, my dear. I want it all or nothing.' She gasped, but he went on unheedingly, 'Oh, you've been a brilliant actress since I apparently shook you out of your self-preoccupation and frightened you into thinking you were going to lose all this . . .'

'*No!*' she cried. 'I haven't, it wasn't . . .'

'Roz, if I thought you were sleeping with someone behind my back I'd probably do something essentially violent. How can you expect me to believe *you* don't give a damn—*if* you feel anything for me at all?'

'I didn't know how you really felt! Adam . . .'

'Then I'll tell you,' he said unpleasantly, 'And for the record, I never realised it so clearly as on that first night in Tokyo when I was tired and depressed and convinced you were drifting further and further away from me whatever I did—and coming to understand what it meant to me. But I persuaded myself to think, what the hell, Roz isn't the only woman in the world, and there's another one right here in this hotel sending out unmistakable signals. Why not avail myself of her?'

Roz stared at him, her face still and pale apart from the streak of dirt on it. 'Did you?' she asked barely audibly.

'I certainly tried to,' he said harshly. 'That I didn't succeed doesn't alter the fact that the intention was there. I'm sure what they say of good intentions applies to the other kind, don't you think?'

'So . . . are you trying to tell me this woman means nothing to you?' she whispered bewilderedly.

'Beyond that she was astonishly understanding where many mightn't have been, no. But what I'm really trying to tell you . . .'

He stopped as silent tears slid down her face, but they were tears of relief and comprehension.

'Roz,' his mouth set in a hard line, 'it's too late for that. I . . .'

'Adam,' she interrupted, wiping the tears away resolutely, 'you said once that we were at cross purposes, but never more so than *now*. Will you let me explain?'

He said nothing, but she thought that he looked fractionally less angry, although his gaze was as sharp as an eagle's and chillingly dispassionate.

She drew a breath. 'Something happened to me too. Something that made me—I don't quite know how to put it into words—afraid. Made me so afraid to fall in love with you that I tried to pretend it wasn't happening to me. It will probably sound crazy to you, and perhaps because it happened when so much had gone wrong for me, it made more of an impression than it should.' She stopped for a moment, then she told him baldly the real reason why the Howards had found her so unsuitable for their son.

He stared at her and she saw the shock in his eyes. Then the almost murderous glint that came to them. 'Roz, why the *hell* didn't you tell me this before?

'I—I didn't even want to think about it,' she stammered. 'It made me feel so awful and . . . cheap, somehow.'

'And *that's* why you married me.'

She managed to smile faintly. 'I'd often wondered what it would be like to be married to you well before that, actually. Do you remember the very first time we met, when I was about fourteen? Well, I used to dream about you for months afterwards.'

'I . . .' Adam started to say something, but it was clear she taken him by surprise again.

'Oh, I'd got over that, or thought I had, but when you asked me to marry you I thought how . . . safe and uncomplicated it sounded—it was more like a business proposition, although you said you found me desirable. That was why I married you. It seemed to cancel out the stigma of . . . of,' her voice cracked, 'other men thinking I was . . . something I had no desire to be. It seemed to offer protection from the kind of agony Mrs Howard was going through. And because I really had no idea what else I could do,' she finished honestly, 'I said yes.'

'But,' she swallowed. 'Subconsciously perhaps, I also vowed to keep it that way—safe and uncomplicated. Nor did I really understand how Mr Howard's view of me had affected my vision of myself, made me determined to stamp out any vague resemblance to the kind of . . . woman he assumed I was, whether in his own defence or not.' She stopped and put a hand up wearily to her face. 'I got terribly mixed up, I suppose you could say. And I was only able to start unravelling it all the night *you* rang me from Tokyo.'

'Go on,' said Adam very quietly.

Roz dropped her hand and straightened her shoulders. 'It . . . that phone call crystallised all the fears I'd had since you'd suggested we have a break from each other.

Together, those two things *were* the turning point, Adam.' She looked at him directly. 'I can't deny it. But they made me understand I'd fallen in love with you, why I'd been fighting you, why I was so terrified to accept how I felt. Also to remember that it hadn't been part of your plan . . .'

He stared at her with the line of his shoulders taut and rigid.

'It certainly hadn't been part of my plan to imagine you in the arms of some lovely geisha and feel like dying,' she confessed huskily.

'I told you—you *told* me, Roz . . .'

'I know.' She smiled sadly. 'All the same, I did. And even if I got the girl wrong . . .'

'You got the scenario right,' he said roughly.

'Perhaps, but I knew I only had myself to blame. You . . .' She stopped and stared down at her hands, then lifted her lashes abruptly. 'You thought I didn't mind what Lucia told me. You were wrong, but I'd already faced it, you see—and done something about it which may not have seemed earth-shattering to you, but it was something I once would never have believed I *could* do. I mean, fight you for the right to love you . . . with my body.'

'You could have told me!'

She stared at him and thought he looked so tall and forbidding, and unmoved. She made a futile little gesture. 'I couldn't prove it then any more than I can now, it seems. I can only say that all this means nothing to me except for the people—Milly, Jeanette, your mother—everyone. They came to mean a lot, such a lot. But I would have gladly even traded them for the ability to bear you a child. I can only say it . . .' She broke off and realised she was crying again, and whirled around suddenly and ran out of the room.

She must have taken him by surprise, because she was out of the house and running through the back garden before he caught her. Then the earth and the sunwarmed grass tilted as she tried to evade him and break free of his arms, but ended up in them and backed up against the trunk of an old gum tree.

Adam stared down at her upturned face and panic-stricken eyes and tightened his arms around her as she moved convulsively. 'Roz—I meant that you should have told me about Mike's father. Because it would have been the best news of my life.'

'But it was so awful!'

'Awful for you, I agree,' he said sombrely, 'but terribly damaging to keep locked up inside you. But at least it explains the damage I *didn't* do with my bloody stupid ideas about love, and that's why it would have been good news.'

Her lips parted, but she couldn't speak.

He went on, 'Roz, I swear the only reason I suggested the break was because I was getting desperate and getting nowhere with you other than seeing you becoming more tense and nervous, so much so it was even affecting you physically.'

'Oh, Adam,' her lips quivered and her voice broke, '*you* could have told me!'

'Unfortunately,' he said with savage mockery, 'that was the last thing I was able to do. Do you remember saying to me once that despite all my cynicism I was determined to make you fall in love with me?'

Roz nodded dazedly after a moment.

'You were right, but not, I realised in a blinding flash when you said it, because I couldn't bear to think of even one woman being unaffected by me, but because I'd fallen in love with you. All the frustration, even the desire to hurt you, added up to one thing suddenly. That was the night I made the decision that perhaps the only chance I had of winning your love was to let you go for a while. Because I knew I couldn't tell you, not me,' he said with a grim little smile. 'It was a miracle I even admitted it to myself, and—well, I've told you how, even after I'd worked it out, I tried to . . . deny it. But admitting it to myself was as far as I was going to go until I was convinced you could love me in return. In the end I have gone further, though.'

'You . . . just now, inside, you looked as if you hated me rather than anything else,' whispered Roz. 'And even when I did start to . . . hope, after you told me about Louise, you were—in between times you were distant, and I thought it was all only an act of kindness on your part. That's why when Lucia told me, it all seemed to fall into place. I thought you must have fallen in love with someone but you couldn't work out what to do with me. And today, I didn't know what to do, how to behave—it was mostly out of fright, terror, the way I was . . .'

'Roz,' he sighed, and swivelled around so that he was leaning against the tree and she was resting against him, 'if I was distant at times, it was because of seeing Louise—no, wait,' he said softly as she tensed, 'let me explain. And coming to understand that my stupid pride was leading me into another trap. Also, coming to realise that I was going to have to lay it down even if you *were* . . . rather brilliantly acting the part of a loving wife because you were afraid of being on your own again. But my pride and I don't part that easily, Roz, and on top of it there was the guilt about Tokyo which you magnified in a curious way.'

She stirred in his arms, 'If—it happened as you say,' she murmured huskily, 'perhaps the intention wasn't really there.'

'Perhaps,' he said with a faint smile twisting his lips. 'Don't think I haven't told myself that. By the way, that was one of the reasons you had to fight so hard to seduce me, something to do with the male psychology, no doubt, particularly the inflated type, like mine,' Adam added wryly.

'What . . . oh, you mean . . .?'

'Mmm. But in the end you . . . restored my confidence beautifully, my darling.'

'I didn't—I had no idea, oh, Adam!' Roz sighed tearfully.

'Don't cry,' he whispered.

'I can't help it, I can't believe . . . I just love you so much . . .'

Presently he said, 'That surprise I brought you from Tokyo—would you like to see it?'

'So it did arrive?' she exclaimed.

'I thought you'd forgotten,' he said ruefully, and kissed her again, but gently.

'No, I thought you had—I didn't know what to think,' Roz confessed.

'Come and see it now,' he invited, releasing her but taking her hand. 'And you might understand why *I* . . . didn't quite know what to think.'

'Oh, Adam!' she breathed minutes later, when his

surprise was all laid out on her bed.

'This, I'm told,' he said gravely, picking up a length of thin silk, 'is a traditional *koshimaki*, and you wear it around your waist in place of underpants. And this is a sort of undershirt...' 'This' was a cotton gauze sort of front-wrap garment. 'Then comes the under-*robe*.' He laid the undershirt back and fingered the splash of yellow silk that lay beside the most exquisite pale pink damask kimono and a brocade obi of gold and silver chrysanthemums.

'Oh, Adam,' said Roz again, 'you bought it for *me*!'

'Yes, but I did have help.' He looked at her straightly.

'I understand,' she said quickly.

'Do you, Roz? She said, after the fiasco and I'd explained some things, that you must be very special and she'd like to help me choose something very special to take home to you. But...' He stopped.

'Then you couldn't give it to me because I reminded you of...?'

'Something like that—my guilt haunting me.'

She moved into his arms. 'Can I try it on? I'm dying to, but I'll have to take these clothes off and...'

'I'll help you.'

'And I should take a shower first because I'm...'

'I'll help you there too,' he said perfectly seriously. 'I'll take a shower with you. You have the most brilliant ideas sometimes.'

'I don't... that wasn't...' Her colour fluctuated and her lips trembled.

'Not the same idea you had about the dining-room table? What a pity,' said Adam very softly and with a smile lurking at the back of his eyes.

'You're never going to let me forget that, are you?' whispered Roz.

'Do you want me to?'

'No. I love you, I love the way you're holding me, and I'd love to do it in the shower ...'

But later, hours later, she stirred in his arms and said, 'Adam, what if we can't have babies?'

He kissed her bare shoulders lingeringly. 'We'll cope,' he murmured. 'We could go a bit dotty and run a zoo or a home for broken-down horses, but so long as we have each other ... But Roz,' he raised his head and pushed himself up on one elbow and stared down at her as he caressed her breasts, 'we've come a long way, and if you can be happy now and at peace with me and with yourself, don't be surprised if we *do*. Would you like to have a small wager with me?'

'No,' she said with a smile. 'I've got the feeling you always win your wagers! I love you ... I can't seem to stop saying that.'

'Don't even try, because——' he paused, then sat up suddenly, and she caught her breath as he exclaimed, 'Bloody hell! That was a *car*. This place is becoming like a railway station! Are you expecting anyone?'

'No.'

'Just don't let it be ...' He slid out of bed and strode over to the window, then swore again. 'I might have known,' he added bitterly.

'Who is it?'

'Mother—and Lucia. Come to try and heal the breach, no doubt. I don't know anyone who has such an annoying, interfering damn family but *this* ...'

'Adam,' Roz broke in, sitting up, 'you mustn't be angry with Lucia.'

'Why shouldn't I be, but I'm going down to tell them . . .'

'No, Adam,' she pleaded, 'you don't understand.'

'. . . to tell them,' he finished, sitting down beside her and gathering her up, 'to stay away for at least six months.'

'But there's something . . .'

He overrode her in a way that made it impossible to speak. He kissed her deeply and urgently and as if it was a matter of extreme urgency for him. So that she forgot what she'd been going to say.

Until he lifted his head at last and released her from the crushing grip he had her in, and said. 'And to tell them that all is well and that nothing will ever again come between me and my geisha.'

NOW ON VIDEO

CLOUD WALTZER

LOVE WITH A PERFECT STRANGER

Copyright reserved © YORKSHIRE TELEVISION LIMITED 1987 ALL RIGHTS RESERVED

Two great Romances available on video... from leading video retailers for just **£9.99** R.R.P.

The love you find in Dreams.

from Autumn 1987

Harlequin Romance movie ™

"TM are trademarks of Harlequin Enterprises B.V., Atlantic Video Ventures authorized user. CIC Video authorized distributor."

Mills & Boon

AND THEN HE KISSED HER...

This is the title of our new venture — an audio tape designed to help you become a successful Mills & Boon author!

In the past, those of you who asked us for advice on how to write for Mills & Boon have been supplied with brief printed guidelines. Our new tape expands on these and, by carefully chosen examples, shows you how to make your story come alive. And we think you'll enjoy listening to it.

You can still get the printed guidelines by writing to our Editorial Department. But, if you would like to have the tape, please send a cheque or postal order for £2.95 (which includes VAT and postage) to:

VAT REG. No. 232 4334 96

AND THEN HE KISSED HER...
To: Mills & Boon Reader Service, FREEPOST, P.O. Box 236, Croydon, Surrey CR9 9EL.

Please send me _____ copies of the audio tape. I enclose a cheque/postal order*, crossed and made payable to Mills & Boon Reader Service, for the sum of £_____ . *Please delete whichever is not applicable.

Signature _____

Name (BLOCK LETTERS) _____

Address _____

_____ Post Code _____

YOU MAY BE MAILED WITH OTHER OFFERS AS A RESULT OF THIS APPLICATION   ED1

The 1987 Christmas Pack

Be swept off your feet this Christmas by Charlotte Lamb's WHIRLWIND, or simply curl up by the fireside with LOVE LIES SLEEPING by Catherine George.

Sit back and enjoy Penny Jordan's AN EXPERT TEACHER, but stay on your guard after reading Roberta Leigh's NO MAN'S MISTRESS.

Four new and different stories for you at Christmas from Mills and Boon.

Available in October Price £4.80

Mills & Boon

Available from Boots, Martins, John Menzies, W. H. Smith, Woolworths and other paperback stockists.